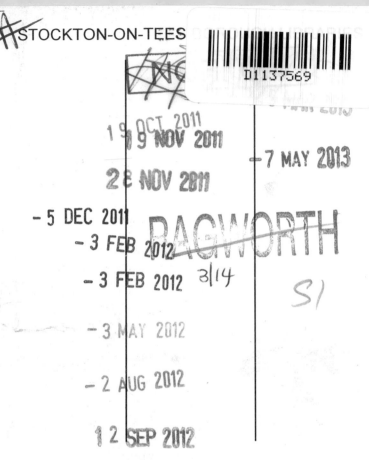
A FINE WILL BE CHARGED IF THE BOOK IS
RETURNED AFTER THE DATE ON WHICH IT IS DUE

This book should be returned on or before the latest date
stamped. It may, if not required by another reader, be
renewed on request for a further loan period.

Kate Hardy lives in Norwich, in the east of England, with her husband, two young children, one bouncy spaniel, and too many books to count! When she's not busy writing romance or researching local history, she helps out at her children's schools. She also loves cooking—spot the recipes sneaked into her books! (They're also on her website, along with extracts and stories behind the books.) Writing for Mills & Boon has been a dream come true for Kate—something she wanted to do ever since she was twelve. She's been writing Medical™ Romances for nearly five years now, and also writes for Mills & Boon® Riva. She says it's the best of both worlds, because she gets to learn lots of new things when she's researching the background to a book: add a touch of passion, drama and danger, a new gorgeous hero every time, and it's the perfect job!

Kate's always delighted to hear from readers, so do drop in to her website at www.katehardy.com

ITALIAN DOCTOR, NO STRINGS ATTACHED

BY
KATE HARDY

All the characters in this book have no existence outside the imagination of the author, and have no relation whatsoever to anyone bearing the same name or names. They are not even distantly inspired by any individual known or unknown to the author, and all the incidents are pure invention.

First published in Great Britain 2011
by Mills & Boon, an imprint of Harlequin (UK) Limited,
Eton House, 18-24 Paradise Road, Richmond, Surrey TW9 1SR

© Pamela Brooks 2011

ISBN: 978 0 263 88606 1

Harlequin (UK) policy is to use papers that are natural, renewable and recyclable products and made from wood grown in sustainable forests. The logging and manufacturing process conform to the legal environmental regulations of the country of origin.

Printed and bound in Spain
by Blackprint CPI, Barcelona

For Michelle

CHAPTER ONE

FACE the fear.

Sydney faced the fear every single day of her life. Every day she made life-or-death decisions. Abseiling down the tower of the London Victoria hospital, to raise funds for specialist equipment for the emergency department, should be a breeze. She had a sheet full of sponsor signatures, with a large amount of money at stake. There was no question that she wouldn't do it. How could she possibly back out now?

But then she looked down. Over the edge. There was a white stone cornice and then...nothing.

For two hundred and fifty feet.

Back in the department, two months ago, this had seemed like a brilliant idea. Right here and now, she knew it was the most stupid, ridiculous thing she'd ever done. She sneaked another look at the edge, hoping that her fairy godmother was passing with some sparkly dust and the drop would look a bit less scary.

It didn't.

And there was no way that she could make herself walk backwards over the edge. OK, so she had a harness on, and a hard hat. The ropes were belayed, or whatever the technical term was, and the experts weren't going to let her fall. She knew that. All she had to do was go backwards over the edge and walk down the building.

But she still couldn't move her feet.

'It's OK, Sydney. You can do it. Just one tiny step back.'

One tiny step backwards. *Over the edge.* She couldn't even reply to the man who'd just spoken to her: the instructor who'd explained carefully to her just what she had to do to get off the top of the tower and go all the way down to the bottom. Her brain was refusing to process his name. Refusing to do anything.

Oh, help.

She couldn't step back. Couldn't step forwards, either, and let the team down.

Why, why, why had she agreed to be the first person down? Whatever had possessed her? Why had she thought it would boost her confidence in herself? She must've been mad. No way could she do this. She was *stuck*.

Then another man joined the instructor at the edge. 'Hi.'

She'd never seen him before. The part of her mind that wasn't completely frozen in fear thought how gorgeous he was, with eyes colour of melted chocolate, dark hair, and an olive complexion. He reminded her a bit of an actor she had a huge crush on and her friends in the department were always teasing her about.

'I'm Marco.'

And his voice was even more gorgeous than his face: just the hint of an accent, incredibly sexy.

He'd introduced himself to her. Now she was supposed to speak. But, just like her feet, her mouth was frozen and it wasn't going to let any proper words out.

'You're Sydney, yes?'

'Uh.'

Clearly he took the little squeak of fear as meaning yes. 'OK. What we're going to do now is sing together, Sydney.'

What? How on earth was *singing* going to help her frozen feet move?

'How about Tom Petty's "Free Falling"?' he suggested.

Not funny. *So* not funny. And just what any of her colleagues would've suggested. Clearly climbing people shared the same kind of dark humour as medics. *Falling.* Uh. She gave him a look of pure loathing.

He grinned. 'At least you're not doing this face down, *tesoro*. That's a bonus. And singing's going to take your mind off it and help you down, I promise.'

He sounded a lot more confident than she felt.

'If I start, will you join in?'

She managed a nod, and in return got a full-wattage smile. If her knees hadn't been frozen, they would definitely have gone weak.

'That's great, *tesoro*. You're going to sing with me. And you're going to keep your right hand behind your back, holding the static line, and just take one tiny step back. You'll feel yourself go down a little bit, but don't worry, that's fine—it's just the tension in the ropes letting you move. The line's going to take your weight. And then you move your right hand out to your side, and it'll give you the slack to start walking down. If you need to stop, just move your hand behind your back again. Got it?'

She nodded again.

'Excellent. Do you know the song "Walking on Sunshine"?'

She could almost hear it in her head, infectious and upbeat, a real summer anthem.

Another nod.

He smiled and began singing. To her amazement, he even hummed the intro, mimicking the tune of the brass section—and then she found herself joining in.

They got to the first chorus. 'One step back,' he encouraged during the bit where he was meant to sing the 'woh-ohs'.

Somehow she did it. Took a step backwards.

Everything lurched, but then it was stable again.

And he was still singing. Still keeping her company. Still with her.

She could do this.

Her voice sounded thready, but she was singing back. And she was walking. Not on sunshine, but against brick.

How she actually got down the building was a blur, but at last she was at the bottom. Her legs were shaking, so were her hands, and she could barely unclip the harness and move out of the way so the next person could abseil down the building and land safely.

'So are you going next?' the instructor asked.

'Me?' It had been a while since Marco had abseiled. But a building in the middle of London was going to be a lot safer than the last abseil he'd done at home, down the cliffs in Capri. Apart from anything else, they didn't have to worry about the tide coming in and causing problems with landing.

He glanced at his watch. Well, it'd be almost as quick as taking the lift. And nobody was going to notice any creases in his suit caused by the abseil harness once they were in the thick of things in the emergency department. 'I'm not on your list,' he warned, 'so it's going to put you off schedule.'

'Not as far off as we would've been if you hadn't talked Sydney down,' the instructor pointed out. 'So are you next?'

He wasn't technically part of the department for another half an hour, and he didn't have a sponsor form; but that wasn't a problem. He'd sponsor himself for the same amount as any of the other registrars had raised. He grinned. 'Yeah, I'm next. Thanks.'

It didn't take long to buckle on the harness. And going over the edge, he felt the whole adrenalin rush as he stepped backwards into nothing... It was the first time he'd really felt alive since Sienna's death.

By the time he reached the bottom of the tower, the rush had filled his entire body.

And the first person he saw when his feet touched the ground was Sydney. The woman he'd talked over the edge. The woman who'd been full of fear, and still looked slightly dazed.

He unbuckled the harness. 'Hey. Are you OK?' he asked softly.

OK? No. Sydney was still shaking all over. 'Yes,' she lied.

Then she made the mistake of looking up. It was him. Mr Gorgeous from the top of the tower. He'd just done exactly what she'd done, and he wasn't a nervous mess. He wasn't even breaking a sweat.

Get a grip, she told herself, and took a deep breath. 'Thanks for talking—well, singing—me down.'

'No problem.' He looked concerned. 'Are you sure you're all right?'

'I have to be—I'm on duty in a few minutes.' And she would be OK. She never let anything get in the way of work.

He touched her face gently with the backs of his fingers. 'I take it this was your first time?'

She nodded. 'And last. Next time one of our consultants gets a bright idea, I'm paying up and bailing out.'

He smiled. 'The adrenalin rush hasn't kicked in yet, then.'

'What adrenalin?'

'Look up,' he said softly.

She did, and saw someone slowly walking backwards over the top of the tower.

'You just did that,' he said.

'And I was stuck. Scared witless. I froze up there.' She shook her head. 'I didn't think I was scared of heights or anything like that. I've never frozen like that before.' Not even when she'd had the MRI scan and they'd told her the bad news. She'd managed to find a bright side. Up there had been simply terrifying.

'But you still did it. Which makes you amazing, in my book.'

'Amazing?' It had been a long, long while since someone had called her amazing.

'Amazing,' he confirmed. 'People like me, who do this for fun—we're not brave. The ones with real courage are people who do it even when they're scared, because they're doing it to make a difference. People like *you*.'

Sydney wasn't sure which one of them moved first, but then his hands were cupping her face and his mouth was brushing lightly against hers. Warm and sweet and promising—and then suddenly it spiralled into something completely different. Something hot and sensual and mind-blowing.

Or maybe that was what he'd meant by 'adrenalin rush'.

When he broke the kiss, she was still shaking—but this time for a different reason. She couldn't remember the last time someone had made her feel like this. And that in itself was incredibly scary.

'Now your eyes are sparkling,' he said softly.

'That's the adrenalin rush,' she said swiftly, not wanting him to think that it was his effect on her.

'Yeah.' He laughed. 'Well. Good to meet you, Sydney. And although I'd love to stay a bit longer and talk, I'd better go, because I'm starting my new job in less than twenty minutes.'

New job? It had to be at the hospital, or he wouldn't have been up the London Victoria's tower in the first place.

'Nice to meet you, too. Good luck with your first shift. Which department are you working in?' she asked.

'Emergency.'

'Me, too.' It suddenly clicked. *Marco*. She'd been too frozen with fear to take it in before. 'You're Dr Ranieri, our new registrar?' The guy on secondment from Rome.

He inclined his head. 'Though I prefer first name terms.'

'Sydney Collins. And I'm a much better doctor than I am an abseiler. Pleased to meet you—properly, this time.' She held her hand out for him to shake.

Clearly she was still wobbly from the abseiling, because her knees went weak again at the touch of his skin against hers and the memory of that kiss made her skin burn.

'So how long have you worked here?' he asked.

'Five years—since I qualified and did my two years' pre-reg training. It's a really nice department to work in. Everyone's great. Except possibly Max Fenton, who suggested we did this abseil in the first place.' She pulled a face. 'I think I've gone off him.'

Marco laughed. 'No, you haven't. He's a nice guy.'

'His wife's nice, too—Marina. Have you met her yet? She's Italian, too. She's working part time at the moment, and then she's off on maternity leave again in a couple of months.' She paused. 'So you've done a lot of climbing and abseiling?'

He shrugged. 'What can I say? I went through a phase of doing extreme sports.'

'You did that sort of thing for *pleasure*? Are you insane?' She shuddered. 'I'm going to have nightmares tonight.'

He just laughed, and Sydney looked at him. He really did have lovely eyes. And a beautiful mouth. Not that she should be thinking about that kiss. It hadn't meant anything; it had just been adrenalin whizzing through her system. She wasn't in the market for a relationship. Not any more. 'Do you sing many people down like that?'

'Not on an abseil, no—it's usually to distract little ones in the department, because it stops them being scared.'

'Fair point.' It was a technique she used, too. 'Though I normally get them to sing "Old Macdonald Had a Farm" or something like that.'

He laughed again. 'Ah, the song choice. I picked that

one because it's a happy song. It always makes me think of driving with the roof down on a summer day.'

Sydney looked at him and took in the quality of his clothes. It was a fair bet that he owned an open-topped sports car. Gorgeous to look at, a nice guy, and beautifully dressed: he was going to have women sighing over him everywhere he walked.

Though not her. She didn't sigh over men, any more. She'd learned the hard way that it wasn't worth the effort: the only person she could really rely on was herself.

'I take it you're meeting Ellen now?' On his first day, of course he'd be meeting the head of the department. At his nod, she said, 'I can show you to her office, if you like.'

'Thanks, that'd be good.'

Sydney Collins was absolutely gorgeous. Chestnut hair cut into a short bob, eyes the colour of the shallow bay near his family home in Capri, and a sweet, heart-shaped face. Better still, she didn't have the 'look at me' attitude that Marco disliked in women who spent hours on their appearance. Now that she wasn't panicking about the abseil, Sydney had turned out to be good company, lively and bright. He liked her instinctively.

And that kiss… He still didn't know why he'd done it; he wasn't in the habit of going round kissing complete strangers. The adrenalin rush from the abseil, maybe. But his mouth was still tingling, and he'd felt that zing between them when she'd shaken his hand. There'd been a look of surprise in her eyes, so he was pretty sure it was a mutual zing.

His head was telling him this was absolutely mad—he

wasn't looking for a relationship. He didn't want one. And yet his heart was saying something else entirely. That he hadn't felt a connection like this for so long: he should seize the moment and put some fun back into his life.

'Here we are,' Sydney said with a smile as they reached Ellen's office. 'No doubt I'll see you in the department later.'

'Sure. Thanks for bringing me here.'

'My pleasure. And thank *you* for getting me off the top of that wretched tower,' she replied. She smiled again, gave him a tiny wave, and headed off to the department.

So, this was it. Meeting the director of the emergency department again, and starting his new job. Six months of working in the busiest department of one of the busiest hospitals in London. And he relished the challenge.

He knocked on Ellen's door.

'Come in,' the director called. She smiled at him when he walked in. 'Have a seat. Was that Sydney I just saw with you?'

'Yes. She showed me the way here.'

'I gather you rescued her earlier.'

He blinked. 'Wow. The hospital grapevine here is *fast*.'

'It certainly is.' Ellen laughed. 'I guess it's one way of meeting your new team. Syd's not a registrar yet, but she's well on the way and she'll be a good support for you.' She gave him a speculative look. 'And I hear you have a good singing voice. You do realise you're going to get nagged into being part of the ED revue if we can get you to extend your secondment and stay past Christmas, don't you?'

He smiled. 'Not a problem. And maybe I can persuade some of the non-singers into forming a choir.'

'I have a feeling you might just manage that.' She smiled at him. 'Come on, let me show you round and introduce you to everyone.'

He'd met half the team when a trolley came round the corner, a paramedic on one side and Sydney on the other; clearly they were heading towards Resus.

He caught snippets of their conversation as the handover continued. 'Knocked off his bike...helmet saved him...broken arm...ribs...'

Given the situation, there was a very high chance that the cyclist would have a pneumothorax. And he'd dealt with enough cycling accidents in his time to be useful here. He glanced at Ellen. 'Mind if I...?'

'I was going to put you on Cubicles, to ease you in gently.' She spread her hands. 'But if you want to hit the ground running, that's fine by me. And you've already met Syd, so I don't have to introduce you. Go for it.'

'Thank you.' He quickened his pace slightly and caught Sydney up. 'Hey. Would another pair of hands be useful right now?'

'Considering that the driver of the car's due in the next ambulance, yes, please,' she said.

Within seconds Marco had swapped his suit jacket for a white coat. Although technically he was the senior doctor, he knew that Sydney had been part of the team for longer and knew her way round. 'I'll follow your lead.'

She looked surprised, and then pleased. 'OK. Thank you.' She turned to their patient. 'Colin, this is Dr Ranieri, our registrar. He's going to help me treat you.

We're going to sort your pain relief first and make you more comfortable, then we can assess you properly.'

He noticed that she didn't use Entonox; clearly she suspected a pneumothorax as well, so she was using a painkiller that wouldn't make the condition worse.

'Where does it hurt most, Colin?' she asked.

'My arm. And my ribs.'

Colin was definitely getting more breathless, Marco noticed, and finding it harder to speak.

Sydney listened to his chest. 'Decreased air entry,' she mouthed to Marco.

'Needle decompression?' he mouthed back.

She nodded.

His first instinct was to offer to do it, but he wanted to see how she worked; besides, given her throwaway comment about being a better doctor than abseiler, he had a feeling she needed to do this—that she needed to prove to him that she was good at her job and not some weak lightweight who couldn't cope. And he could always step in if she needed help.

'I'll hand you the stuff and keep an eye on the monitors,' he said.

'Thanks. Colin, I know you're finding it hard to breathe, so I'm going to put an oxygen mask on you to make it easier for you.' Gently, she put the mask on. 'At the moment, you've got air moving into the space around your lungs and it's causing pressure. I need to take it off; that means I'm going to have to put a needle in, but it's not going to hurt. Is that OK?'

Colin gave a weary nod.

Marco handed her a cannula.

'Thanks, Marco.' She smiled in acknowledgement,

and for a second Marco was lost in a mad memory about what her mouth had felt like against his.

But this wasn't the time or the place to think about that. They had a seriously ill patient who needed their help.

She inserted the cannula in the second intercostal space, withdrew the needle and listened for the hiss of gas. 'Great, that's it,' she said. 'Colin, now I need to put a chest drain in, to take off any fluid and gases that shouldn't be there and keep you comfortable.' She explained the procedure swiftly to him. 'I'm going to give you extra pain relief so you're not going to feel anything, but I need your consent for me to treat you.'

Colin lifted the mask away. 'Do whatever you have to. I'm in your hands,' he mumbled.

'OK, sweetheart. I promise I'm going to be as gentle as I can.'

Stella, one of the senior nurses, cleaned Colin's skin and covered it with sterile drapes. Marco handed Sydney the syringe and she injected local anaesthetic, prepared the chest drain and then inserted it. He was impressed by how smoothly and confidently she did it; Ellen had been spot on in her assessment of the younger doctor's skills.

He kept an eye on the monitors. 'Heart and BP are both fine. Do you want me to write up the notes as you do the assessment?'

'That'd be good. Thanks.'

She checked Colin over very gently and Marco wrote up the notes as she went. 'Suspected multiple rib fractures,' she said, 'but no sign of a flail segment. That's good news, Colin.' She checked the distal pulses and the sensation in his broken arm. 'I think you've fractured your elbow, so I'm going to refer you to our orthopaedic surgeon to fix that for you.' Finally, she took a sample for blood gases.

'OK, Colin, I'm all done here. I'm going to send you for chest X-ray so we can check out your ribs; I think you've broken several, but hopefully they're not complicated breaks. I also want to check out your arm properly for the surgeon. Is there anyone we can call for you while you're in X-Ray?'

'My wife, Janey.' He rattled off a number, which Marco wrote down.

'I'll call her,' Sydney promised.

'And I'll take you to X-Ray,' Marco said.

'Do you know where it is?' Sydney mouthed, so Colin couldn't see.

'I can read the signs,' Marco mouthed back with a grin.

She gave him the cheekiest wink he'd ever seen, and he was still smiling by the time he got to the X-ray department.

She was working on the driver of the car when he got back to Resus, and sent him off for observation for possible concussion. By the time she'd finished, Colin's X-rays were ready on the system for review.

'Want to look at these with me?' she asked.

'Sure.'

She peered closely at the screen. 'Hmm. Not all fractures show up on a chest X-ray, but it looks as if I'm right and it's not flail chest, so that's a good start.' She grimaced at the X-ray of Colin's elbow. 'That's a mess. It's going to need fixators. I'll refer him to the orthopods and warn them that he's already had a pneumothorax.'

She went back over to Colin. 'I've had a look at the

X-rays. The good news is that your ribs will heal by themselves, though it's going to be a bit painful for you over the next few days. But your elbow's going to need pinning, so I'm going to take you out to one of the cubicles to wait for the orthopaedic surgeon, and he'll take you to Theatre to fix your arm.'

Colin removed the oxygen mask. 'Janey?'

'She's on her way. And if you're already in Theatre by the time she gets here, our receptionists know to call me, and I'll take her up to the right waiting area and make sure she's looked after.'

'Thank you.' His voice sounded choked. 'I…'

She laid her hand on his uninjured arm to reassure him. 'It's OK. That's what I'm here for. You're going to be sore for a while, but it could've been an awful lot worse. Everything's going to be fine now,' she soothed.

The rest of the shift was equally busy, and Marco thoroughly enjoyed the rush and the challenge. Moving to London for six months was the best thing he could've done. There were no memories here, no ghosts to haunt him. And maybe, just maybe, he could finally start to move on with his life after two years of being numbed by guilt.

At the end of the shift, he saw Sydney outside the restroom. 'Hi.'

'Hi.' She smiled at him. 'So did you enjoy your first day?'

'Yes. You were right—it's a nice department.' He smiled back. 'And you're definitely a better doctor than you are an abseiler.' He'd liked the way she worked: confident, efficient, but most importantly putting the patients first and making them comfortable. Her people skills were top-notch. 'I was wondering—are you busy?'

She looked slightly wary. 'Busy?'

'If you're not, I thought maybe we could do something tonight.'

Her expression grew warier still. 'What, a welcome to the team thing?'

'No, just you and me.' He paused. There was a question he really had to ask before this went any further. 'Unless you have a significant other?'

CHAPTER TWO

SYDNEY'S head was telling her that this was a bad, bad idea. Going out with Marco—just the two of them. But she couldn't get that kiss out of her head. The way he'd made her feel, those little sparkles of pleasure running through her as his mouth had moved over hers. Maybe it was the adrenalin rush from the abseil still scrambling her common sense, but it had been too long since she'd let herself have fun.

He was only going to be at the London Victoria for six months. And he was asking her out on a date, not suggesting a long-term commitment. So on a need-to-know basis he didn't actually have to know about her neurofibromatosis, did he?

There was only one other reason she could think of why she ought to say no. 'We work together. It's usually not a good idea to date someone in your department,' she hedged. 'Things can get a bit—well, awkward.'

'We're both adults,' he said softly, 'and I think we can be professional enough to keep what happens outside work completely separate from what happens inside work.' He paused, keeping eye contact. 'So will you have dinner with me tonight?'

Clearly the adrenalin from the abseil was still

affecting her head, because Sydney found herself returning his smile. 'Thank you. I'd like that.'

'How about we go out now, straight from work?' he suggested. 'Then neither of us has to go home, dress up and drag ourselves out again.'

She looked at him with raised eyebrows. 'Marco, you're already way more dressed up than anyone else in the department. I hate to think what your definition of "dressing up" might be.'

He laughed. 'Before they retired, my parents designed clothes. My older brother and sister run the business now, and they tend to use me as a clothes horse—which is fine by me, because it means I never have to drag myself round the clothes shops, and my wardrobe's always stocked.'

'What happens if they give you something you really hate wearing?' she asked, sounding curious.

'They only did that when I dated their favourite model,' he said. 'To make the point that they didn't approve.'

'So you're an Italian playboy,' she teased.

'Sometimes,' he teased back. 'Actually, I'm starving. Where do you recommend we go?'

'Normally if I go straight from work it's to a pizza place or a trattoria.' She raised an eyebrow. 'Not that I'd dare suggest either of those to an Italian.'

He laughed. 'I'm not *that* fussy.'

'Do you like Chinese food?'

'I love it.'

'Good. Then I know just the place.'

The restaurant wasn't in the slightest bit romantic; it was very workmanlike, with bright lighting, but the food was terrific and Marco was glad that she'd suggested sharing several dishes. Well, apart from the fact that their hands kept accidentally meeting as they served themselves, because the touch of her skin against his was sending little flashes of desire up and down his spine—desire he hadn't felt in a long, long time. He had a feeling that she was affected in just the same way, because her pupils were huge; in this harsh lighting, he'd expect them to be almost pinpoint.

He really hadn't expected this. He couldn't even remember the last time he'd felt this attracted to someone. The times he'd dated during the past year had been in a failed attempt to forget Sienna, and the relationships had fizzled out by the end of the second date.

But there was something about Sydney. Something that felt different. Something that intrigued him and made him want to know more.

'So are you enjoying London?' she asked.

'Very much.'

'What made you decide to come to England?'

'It was a good opportunity,' Marco prevaricated. He could hardly tell her the truth—that he'd needed to get away from Rome. Away from the memories, away from the guilt. Two years of toughing it out had just worn him down, and all that trying hadn't stopped the bad feelings. At least here he didn't have to think about it all the time. He could simply block it out, because he and Sienna had never been to London and there were no memories of her here to haunt him. 'It's one of the busiest departments in one of the busiest hospitals in London. It'll be good experience for me and, when I go back to Rome, I'll have a better chance of promotion.'

Last time he'd been promoted, it had ended in heartache. In his life falling apart completely. Next time, he was determined it would be different.

He kept the conversation light until the meal had ended. 'Can I see you home?' he asked.

Her eyes widened slightly. Fear? he wondered. But why would she be afraid of him? Worried that he was taking this too fast, maybe?

'That wasn't a clumsy way of saying I'm expecting you to take me to bed just because I took you out to dinner tonight,' he said softly. 'You're female, and you had dinner with me, so I need to see you home safely. That's all.'

That made her smile. 'That's very gallant of you. Old-fashioned, even.'

'It's how I was brought up.'

'Nice manners. I like that.' She bit her lip. 'And thank you.'

He frowned. 'For what?'

'For not taking this thing between us too fast. I'm...' She took a deep breath. 'I'm not really used to dating. I've been focused on my career.'

'I'm not really used to dating, either.' He'd been in a relationship with the same woman since he was eighteen. Since his first day at university. Until the day two years ago when he'd taken that phone call and his world had fallen apart. 'And I've just started a new job in a new hospital.'

'And a new country,' she finished.

He nodded. 'So. This thing between you and me—no pressure. We'll just see where it takes us, yes?'

'Thank you. That works for me,' she said softly.

When they reached her flat, she looked at him. 'If you want to come in for a coffee, you're welcome.'

'Coffee meaning *just* coffee,' he checked.

She smiled, and he was glad to see a tiny bit of the wariness fade from her eyes. So had she had a bad experience with someone who'd pushed her too far, too fast? Was that why she avoided dating and concentrated on her career—why she'd thanked him for not taking this too fast? Not that it was any of his business; and now really wasn't the right time to ask.

He followed her into the kitchen, noting that her flat was small but neat. There were lots of photographs everywhere, and they were people who looked quite like her; clearly she was as close to her family as he was to his. Another thing they had in common.

'I'm afraid it's only instant coffee,' she said as she switched the kettle on.

'Instant's fine.'

She gave him a sidelong look. 'I bet you only have fresh coffee at your place.'

He laughed. 'Yes. But I've been either a medical student or a doctor for sixteen years, so I've learned not to be too particular. Coffee's coffee.'

'I do have something to go with it.' She rummaged in the fridge and produced a box. 'My bad habit.'

'Chocolate?'

'Better than chocolate,' she said with a smile.

He looked more closely at the packaging, and smiled as he recognised it. One of his own bad habits, too. 'Gianduja. I'm impressed. You're a woman of taste.'

She gestured to him to sit down at her kitchen table, and put some music on: a solo female singer, backed by guitar and piano, gentle stuff that he rather liked.

'How do you like your coffee?'

'Strong, no milk, please.'

She handed him a mug, and sat down next to him. But then they reached for a piece of gianduja at the same time and their fingers touched. He saw the sudden shock in her eyes, the way her mouth parted as if inviting a kiss.

And he really, really wanted to kiss her. Just like he had after the abseil. He needed to feel her mouth beneath hers, warm and soft and sweet and generous.

Except she'd thanked him earlier for not taking things too fast.

So, instead, he took her hand, pressed a kiss into her palm and folded her fingers over it.

'What was that for?' she asked. The wariness was back in her eyes.

'Because I'm trying very hard not to take this too fast,' he said. 'This is a compromise. A kiss that won't scare you off.' A kiss that wouldn't scare him off, either, if he was honest about it. The way she made him feel was unsettling, something he really wasn't used to. His head was telling him that this was a seriously bad idea; did he really want to put himself back in a position where he could lose someone? Hadn't he already learned that the hard and painful way? And yet there was something about her he couldn't resist. Her warmth. Her sweetness.

Colour bloomed in her cheeks. 'I feel like such a wimp.'

'About this morning. Just so you know,' he said, 'I don't make a habit of going around kissing complete strangers.'

'Neither do I.' The colour in her cheeks deepened. 'And I kissed you back.'

And he could see in her eyes that she'd enjoyed it as

much as he had. That she, like him, had mixed feelings: part of her wanted to see where this took them, and part of her wanted to run back to her safety zone. 'Tell me,' he coaxed gently. 'You feel the same thing, don't you? Something you weren't expecting or looking for, and maybe it scares the hell out of you because your head's saying you don't need the complications. But it's there and you can't get me out of your head—just as I can't get you out of mine, and I've been thinking about you ever since I first met you.'

He could see in her expression that she was thinking about denying it; but then she gave in. 'Yes,' she admitted, her voice husky. 'To all of that.'

He stroked the backs of her fingers with the pad of his thumb. 'I like you, Sydney. You're calm and you're good with the patients. I like that. And you're good company—well, when you're not stuck on an abseiling rope.'

She groaned. 'I'm never going to live that down, am I?'

'If I hadn't seen it for myself, I would've said it was a vicious rumour. Someone as calm and confident and efficient as you, panicking. But it's nice to know you're not really superwoman. That you have panicky moments, like the rest of us.'

She blinked. 'You're telling me that *you* have panicky moments? I'm not buying that one. I've worked with you. OK, so you let me lead, this afternoon, but we both know you have more experience than I do. You were being nice and trying to restore my confidence after the abseil.'

Oh. So she'd picked that up. 'Mmm,' he admitted.

'And I appreciated it. Because it worked.'

'Good.' He paused. 'Do you trust me as a doctor?'

'Yes.'

'Well, that's a start. And so's this.' He leaned forward and touched his mouth to hers. Briefly. Sweetly.

And the second he felt her lips part slightly, he was lost. He couldn't pull away. He gave in to the desperate need to kiss her properly. Within moments, she was kissing him back, her hands were cradling his face, and it felt as if stars were exploding in his head.

When he finally broke the kiss, they were both shaking.

This really wasn't supposed to happen, Sydney thought. *I wasn't supposed to be attracted to him. This was meant to be just putting a bit of fun back into my life. Seizing the moment. Enjoying a casual date. And now I'm way out of my depth, because I want this to go further—a lot further—and I think he feels the same way.*

Which means I'm going to have to tell him the truth about me.

Ice trickled down her spine. Down the scar. The physical reminder of the thing that had smashed up her marriage. The thing that had stopped her having a relationship since her marriage had broken up, because the scar on her back and the ugly patch of skin on her arm were constant reminders of Craig's betrayal and the reasons behind it, making her want to keep her distance. And there was no way she could bluff her way through it, because if she went to bed with Marco it would mean getting naked. That he'd touch her. Look at her. He'd either feel the scar tissue or see it for himself—and then he'd ask questions. Of course he would. Anyone would be curious. And then…oh, hell, then she'd have to be honest.

She really owed it to him to be honest now. So he knew exactly what he was getting into, if he started seeing her.

But the words stuck miserably in her throat and refused to come out.

'I'm sorry,' he said softly. 'Well, I'm not sorry for kissing you. I enjoyed it. But I *am* sorry for pushing you out of your comfort zone, for taking this faster than you're happy with.'

'I'm sorry, too,' she whispered. 'For—for being such a coward.'

He stroked her face. 'You're not a coward. I'm rushing you. So I'll go home now.' He took her hand again, kissed her palm and folded her fingers over his kiss, just as he had before. 'And I'll see you at work tomorrow.'

'OK.' She took a deep breath. 'Thank you for this evening. I enjoyed it.'

'So did I.' The expression in his eyes was so sweet, so gentle, that Sydney was close to tears. She ached to be able to trust. To be normal. To be whole.

But that wasn't going to happen. And somehow, she was going to have to find the right words to tell him tomorrow at work.

The truth.

CHAPTER THREE

'HEY, Syd!' One of the junior doctors met Marco and Sydney in the corridor on their way to Cubicles the next morning. 'Got a question for you. Who's the abseilers' favourite singer?' He grinned, looking pleased with himself. '*Cliff* Richard.'

She rolled her eyes. 'Pete, that's terrible.'

He laughed. 'I'll pay up my sponsorship at lunchtime.'

'Yes, and you can pay double if you make any more abseiling jokes,' she threatened, laughing back. 'Though I've got one for you. Two drums and a cymbal abseiled down a cliff. Boom, ba-doom, tssssh.'

'Oh, that's brilliant.' Pete gave her a high five. 'If I have any kids on my list today, I'm *so* going to use that one.'

Yet more things to like about her, Marco thought. Sydney didn't overreact to good-natured teasing, and she thought on her feet. The more he saw of her, the more he liked.

He knew that she liked him, too, from the way she'd responded to his kiss last night. Then something had spooked her. Bad memories, maybe? Perhaps he could get her to open up to him.

Though that made him the biggest hypocrite in the

world, because no way was he planning to open up and talk about Sienna.

Later, he told himself. Work, first.

Their first patient that morning was an elderly woman complaining of abdominal pain. It was a symptom common to a very wide range of conditions, making it difficult to diagnose what the problem was.

'Mrs Kane, I'm Marco Ranieri and this is Sydney Collins,' he said. 'We're going to find out what's making your stomach hurt, and make you much more comfortable. How long have you been feeling like this?'

'A couple of days. I wasn't going to bother you, but then it started hurting when the postman came, and he called the ambulance.'

'May we examine you?' he asked. 'We'll be as gentle as we can, if you can tell us where it hurts most.'

'Yes,' she whispered.

Gently, Marco examined her. There wasn't any guarding or localised tenderness: just general abdominal pain.

Sydney checked her temperature. 'You don't have any sign of fever, Mrs Kane.'

Which ruled out a couple of things, but he still had a few questions. 'I know this is personal, and I'm sorry, but may I ask when you last went to the toilet and passed a stool?'

Mrs Kane thought about it. 'A couple of days ago. I tried yesterday and couldn't,' she said.

Constipation could cause stomach pain; but Marco instinctively knew it wasn't that. There was more she wasn't telling them.

'Can I ask what you've eaten lately?'

Mrs Kane made a face. 'I haven't really been hungry.'

'Have you been sick at all, Mrs Kane?' Sydney asked.

'No. I thought I was going to be, yesterday, but then I had a drink of water and I was all right.'

'Again, I apologise for the personal question, but have you needed to wee more often?' Sydney asked.

'A bit.' Mrs Kane wrinkled her nose. 'But that's my age, isn't it?'

'Could be,' Sydney said with a smile. She caught Marco's eye. 'Quick word?' she mouthed.

'Mrs Kane, we just need to check something out, and then we'll come back to see you, if that's OK?' Marco asked.

At her nod, he followed Sydney out of the cubicle.

'I know appendicitis is much more common in teenagers and young adults, but I have a feeling about this,' Sydney said.

'I agree. The presentation of appendicitis doesn't tend to be typical in very young or elderly patients—and if her appendix is retrocaecal, then it won't show up as pain moving from around her navel to the right iliac fossa.'

'And needing to wee more frequently—it could be an inflamed appendix irritating her ureter.'

'We're going to have to do a PR exam,' Marco said.

'It'd be more tactful if I do it,' Sydney said.

'Do you mind?'

She shrugged. 'That's what teamwork's for. Keeping our patient as comfortable as possible.'

They went back into the cubicle. 'Mrs Kane, we need to give you an internal exam,' Marco said, 'and then maybe a blood test and possibly a scan to give us a better idea of what's causing your pain—we want to rule out a couple of possibilities.' Diverticulitis and cancer were uppermost in his mind, though he wasn't going to alarm his patient by mentioning them at this stage.

'As an internal exam's a bit personal,' Sydney said. 'Would you prefer me to do it?'

Mrs Kane looked grateful. 'Thank you.'

'Marco, if you can excuse us a moment?' she asked.

'Of course. Give me a shout when you need me,' Marco said, and left the cubicle.

'Ow, that makes my tummy hurt,' Mrs Kane said during the exam.

Bingo: just what Sydney had expected to hear. 'Sorry, I wasn't intending to make it hurt. Let's make you more comfortable.' She helped the elderly lady restore order to her clothes and sit up. 'I think your appendix is inflamed and we're going to need to take it out.' She wasn't going to worry Mrs Kane by telling her, but elderly people were more prone to complications—and there was a higher risk of dying from a perforated appendix. 'Though sometimes we suspect appendicitis and it turns out that the appendix is perfectly healthy, so before I send you off to the surgeon I want to do a couple more tests, if that's OK?'

'Are they going to hurt?'

'You might feel a scratch when I take some blood,' Sydney said, 'but the scan definitely won't hurt.'

The blood tests came back with a high white cell count, and the CT scan showed Marco and Sydney exactly what they'd expected. 'Definitely an inflamed appendix,' Marco said.

They reassured Mrs Kane that the operation was done by keyhole surgery nowadays, so she'd recover relatively quickly, and introduced her to the surgeon, who also spent time reassuring her before taking her up to Theatre himself.

'Good call,' Marco said to Sydney.

'Thanks, but I could've been wrong—you know as well as I do how difficult it is to diagnose abdominal pain in elderly patients.' She shrugged. 'I just happened to read a few journal articles about it recently and they stuck in my mind.'

'Still a good call,' he said with a smile.

There was barely time for a break during the day; at the end of their shift, Marco caught Sydney just as she was leaving the hospital. 'What shift are you on tomorrow?'

'Late,' she said.

'Me, too.' He smiled at her. 'Do you fancy going to the cinema tonight?'

This was where she should make some excuse. Especially as she still hadn't found the right words to tell him about her condition.

But would it really hurt to see a film with him? And maybe afterwards they could talk. Was it so wrong of her to want just a couple more hours of fun, of enjoying his company, of enjoying being someone's girlfriend again? 'That'd be lovely.'

He took out his mobile phone and pulled the local cinema's details onto the screen. 'Drama or comedy?'

Given what she was going to tell him tonight, she could do with some light relief first. 'Comedy—if that's OK with you.'

'It's fine.' He consulted the screen. 'It starts at eight. Pick you up at half seven?'

'I've got a few things to sort out at home. Can I meet you there at quarter to?'

He smiled. 'Sure. I'll buy the tickets and you buy the popcorn.'

She smiled back. 'Deal.'

Even though the film was one she'd wanted to see and starred one of her favourite actors, Sydney found it hard to concentrate. Firstly because she still hadn't worked out a gentle way of telling him about the neurofibromatosis, and secondly because they'd finished the popcorn and Marco was holding her hand.

Just holding her hand.

How could such a light, gentle contact set all her nerve endings tingling? How could it make her whole body feel liquid with desire? How?

By the time they got back to her flat, Sydney was almost quivering with need.

She had to tell him. Now. Before things went any further. It wasn't fair to let him think there could be any possibility of a future between them, when she knew she had nothing to offer him.

'Marco—' she began as she opened her front door.

'I know,' he said softly.

He knew? What? How could he possibly know? The only people at work who knew about her condition were Ellen and the consultants, and there was no way they would've broken her confidence.

And then she stopped thinking as Marco cupped her face with his hands and brought his mouth down on hers. His kiss was soft, sweet and coaxing; every movement of his lips against hers made the blood feel as if it were fizzing through her veins. All thoughts of telling him were gone—until he untucked her shirt from her jeans and slid his hands underneath the hem, his fingertips moving in tiny circles across her back.

The second he touched scar tissue, he stopped. Pulled back. Looked at her, his eyes full of questions. 'Sydney?'

She blew out a breath and pulled away from him, wrapping her arms round herself like a shield. 'I'm sorry,' she whispered. 'I should've told you. I meant to tell you, but...' Her voice faded. How stupid she was to have wanted something she couldn't have. Hadn't she learned from the mess of her marriage to Craig? Her husband hadn't been able to cope with her condition; even though Marco was a doctor, would understand it more, it was still a big ask.

She closed her eyes, not wanting to see pity on Marco's face when she told him. And opened them again when he picked her up, carried her into the living room and sat on the sofa, settling her on his lap. 'Marco?' she asked, not understanding why he was still there. Shouldn't he be backing away as fast as he could?

'That feels like scar tissue,' he said softly. 'And, no, you don't have to tell me about it if you don't want to. I just wanted to be sure that I hadn't hurt you.'

It was the last thing she'd expected to hear, and it took her breath away.

'Sydney?' His voice was so gentle that it brought tears to her eyes—tears she quickly blinked away. She wasn't this weak, pathetic, needy creature. She was a strong woman. A damn good doctor. She'd just made the mistake of forgetting who she was for a little while and wanting something normal. 'No, you didn't hurt me. But thank you for—' The words caught in her throat for a moment. 'For being kind.'

'Kind isn't *quite* the way I feel,' he said.

'I meant to tell you.' She shook her head. 'Sorry. It was unfair of me to agree to date you.'

'Unfair?' He looked puzzled. 'How?'

'Because we can't really see where this thing takes us. I owe it to you to tell the truth—but I'd appreciate it if it didn't go any further than you.'

'Of course.' He frowned. 'You don't owe me anything, Sydney. But if you want to talk, I'm listening.'

She took a deep breath. 'I have neurofibromatosis type two. NF2 for short.'

He stroked her face. 'I'm an emergency specialist. I'm sorry, I don't know anything about NF2. What is it?'

'It's a genetic problem with chromosome 22,' she explained. 'It causes benign tumours to grow on nerve cells and the skin. And although it does run in families, it can also just happen out of nowhere, a mutation in the genes that takes years to show up.'

'One of your parents has it?' he guessed.

She shook her head. 'Neither of them are carriers, and my brother and sister had the tests—they're both fine. It's just me.' And how she'd raged about the unfairness of it, when she'd learned about her condition. One in forty thousand people had it. Why her? What had she done to deserve it?

Then the practical side of her had taken over, kicking out the pointless self-pity. Whining about it wasn't going to change anything. The best thing she could do was make herself informed, to understand what the condition was and how she could work round it to live as normal a life as possible.

'That's pretty tough on you,' he said.

'I'm fine,' she said, knowing it wasn't strictly true.

'So how did you find out?'

'I had back pain and nothing helped. Eventually I had an MRI scan to see if there were any lesions, and that's when they discovered the tumours pressing on my spine.' One of them had been the size of a grapefruit; and the operation had meant that she'd had to take some of her finals papers from her hospital bed. Not that she was going to tell Marco about that; she didn't want his pity.

'Which is why I felt the scar tissue on your back just now,' he said softly.

'Yes. The surgeon operated to remove the tumours, and they haven't grown back yet.' She dug her nails into her palm, reminding herself not to get emotional about it. OK, so the condition was incurable, but it wasn't terminal. It could be much, much worse; it just made her life a bit awkward, from time to time.

And it had blown her marriage apart.

'Are the tumours likely to grow back or cause you problems again?'

'Maybe; maybe not. I get a check-up every year to see how things are. I have a small schwannoma—what they used to call an acoustic neuroma—on both vestibular nerves, but the schwannomas are growing really slowly and they're not causing me tinnitus or anything, so my specialist says we'll keep on with a conservative approach.' She shrugged. 'So I'm fine.'

To her shock, he brushed his mouth against hers.

'What was that for?'

'For being brave,' he said simply. 'For telling me. And it won't go any further.'

And neither would their relationship.

She would've climbed off his lap, except his arms

were still wrapped tightly round her. She frowned. 'Marco?' Wasn't this the bit where he was supposed to walk out?

He kissed her lightly again. 'This doesn't change anything between us, Sydney.'

'Doesn't it?'

'No.'

She couldn't quite take it in. It had changed everything between her and Craig. Changed all their plans. Especially when they'd seen the genetic counsellor. Craig had panicked that the baby would inherit her condition; the counsellor had said that they could go for IVF and screen the embryo before implantation to make sure the baby hadn't inherited the chromosomal problem. Or there were other options: adoption, fostering. They could still have a family.

But Craig had stopped touching her after that day. Not just because of the risk of an accidental pregnancy: he'd called Sydney selfish for wanting a baby at all, because the chances were that her condition would worsen during pregnancy. The way he saw it, he'd be left carrying the burden of childcare and looking after her, too.

His voice echoed in her head. *You're so selfish. You haven't thought how it would affect me—how it would affect our baby. All you can think about is your need for a child.*

A child they'd both wanted. Or so she'd thought at the time.

She'd tried talking to him about adoption, but by then he'd looked things up on the internet, seen the worst-case scenarios and panicked. *How do you know the tumours won't turn malignant and you'll die? And then how am I going to be able to work* and *look after a child?*

He'd countered every argument she had. And then he'd moved into the spare bedroom, saying that he couldn't bear the sight of her arm. It had taken Sydney a long, long time to realise that it wasn't just because her skin was ugly enough to disgust him: for Craig, too, it was a physical reminder of their situation, and he simply hadn't been able to cope with it. And although she hadn't been too surprised when he'd moved out, she'd been shocked to hear his news only a matter of weeks later. News that felt as if someone had reached inside her, gripped her heart in an iron fist and ripped it out of her.

And she would never put herself in a position where someone could hurt her like that again.

'Sydney.' Marco's voice was soft. 'I take it that it did make a difference to someone else?'

She didn't want to talk about Craig. Not now. 'What makes you say that?'

'Because the sparkle's gone from your eyes. As if you're remembering something painful. Something someone said to you, something someone did, maybe. I'm not going to pry.' He kissed her lightly. 'But I'd like to see that sparkle back. The sparkle that was there last night when I kissed you, and tonight when we walked out of the cinema.'

A sparkle that had been there because, for those brief moments, she'd forgotten who and what she was.

Marco was being kind. But she was going to have to face the truth, and there was only one way to do that. Head on. She unbuttoned her shirt and slipped it down over her arm to reveal the large patch of skin covered with tiny nodules.

This was the bit where he'd walk away.

Marco could see it in her face: she was expecting him to be disgusted. To walk away. To fail the challenge.

So his guess had been right. Someone had hurt her badly. And Marco guessed that it went deeper than just that patch of skin. The man had clearly made her feel worthless as well as ugly.

'That's it?' he asked.

'Yes.'

Her eyes were a little over-bright, and he guessed that she was reliving past memories. And yet it was only a small part of her. Something that didn't bother him.

Gently, he reached out and stroked her skin. 'Does it hurt if I do this?'

'No.' Though her lower lip wobbled slightly, as if she was biting back the tears.

'Good. What about this?' He touched his mouth to the area where the nodules were.

'No.' Her voice was shaky, and he glanced up to discover that a single tear had spilled over her lashes and was rolling down her face.

'Ah, *tesoro*. I didn't mean to make you cry. I just wanted to show you that...' He shook his head. 'That this doesn't matter. It's surface. Moles, skin tags, birth marks, port wine stains—they're all common enough.'

She said nothing, but he'd seen the flicker of past pain in her expression. Whatever the guy had said to her, it had really hurt her. And it was about more than just her appearance, he'd guess. He would've liked to shake the guy, break his nose—except that wouldn't solve anything or make Sydney feel better.

He tried again. 'Nobody's perfect. Even a newborn baby often has milk spots or stork marks.'

'But not like this. It's *ugly*.'

That definitely didn't sound like the confident, bright doctor he knew from work; those were someone else's words. Her ex had clearly chipped away at her self-belief. 'Actually, no—it's just part of you. Just like a port wine stain would be.' And anyone who cared about her would accept it, not make a big deal out of it the way her ex obviously had.

He brushed his mouth against hers, and gently helped her back into her shirt. 'Just so you know, I'm not covering your arm up because I don't want to look at you or touch you—because I do want to look at you, Sydney. I do want to touch you. I'm covering you up for one reason only, and that's because right now I can see that you're uncomfortable with your skin being bared. I don't want you to be uncomfortable. I want you to be relaxed with me.'

She swallowed hard. 'I'm sorry. I'm being wet.'

'No. I've clearly brought some bad memories back to you, and I'm sorry for that.' He stroked her face. 'I'd guess that the person you should've been able to rely on let you down—and I'd guess it was when you were at your most vulnerable, say when you first found out that you had NF2.'

'Something like that,' she admitted. 'Though not when I first found out. Later.'

'I'm sorry he wasn't the man you deserved. But it's his loss, not yours.' Marco felt his lip curl in disgust. 'There's more to you than just your skin and your NF2, and beauty's much more than skin-deep.' He tightened his arms round her. *'Non tutti i mali vengono per nuocere.'*

'I don't speak Italian,' she said, 'so you've lost me there.'

'Every cloud has a silver lining,' he translated. 'We're both free. So there's no reason why we can't see where this takes us.'

'And this…' she gestured to her arm, though he guessed that really she meant the whole condition '…*really* doesn't matter?'

'It really doesn't matter,' he confirmed. Though there was one thing he needed to know. 'You said the tumours are benign. So it's not terminal.'

'Incurable, but not terminal,' she confirmed. 'And not contagious, either.' She took a deep breath. 'Though there's a fifty per cent chance of passing it on to a child. Just as well I don't ever want children.'

Her voice was light, but he'd seen something briefly in her eyes before she'd masked it—something that told him that it was a little more complicated than that. Just as it was for him; if things had gone to plan, he would've been a father now. Sienna would've been on maternity leave with their first baby.

It wasn't going to happen now, so there was no point in dwelling on just how much he'd lost. 'Noted,' he said softly. 'So if this thing between us takes us where I think it's going—where I'd like it to go—we'll be careful. Very, very careful.'

She looked completely taken aback. 'You want to…' she paused, as if searching for the right words '…go to bed with me?'

He could tell her in words, but he had a feeling that

the way her ex had undermined her would mean she'd find it difficult to believe him. So maybe there was a better way of explaining. He shifted her slightly on his lap, so she could feel his arousal for herself. 'Does that answer your question?' he asked.

Colour bloomed in her face. 'Oh.'

'Good.' He caught her lower lip briefly between his. 'But I'm not going to rush you into anything tonight. Let's have fun getting to know each other.'

For a moment, he thought she was going to back away. But then she stroked his face, a look of wonder in her eyes. 'Yes.'

He stole a kiss. 'You won't regret this, *tesoro*,' he promised. He'd make sure of that. 'And now, I'm going home. While I still have a smidgen of self-control left. Because, even though I'd really like to take you to bed right now, I think you need a little more time to get used to the idea.'

She nodded. 'I'm sorry.'

'Don't apologise. It's not a problem.' He kissed her again. 'I'll see you tomorrow. *Buona notte.*'

CHAPTER FOUR

THE next day, Sydney was smiling all the way in to work; butterflies were doing a happy dance in her stomach at the thought of seeing Marco. She still couldn't quite believe that someone as gorgeous as Marco had even given her a second glance, let alone wanted a relationship with her. Especially now he knew the truth about her. Yet there had been no pity in his eyes when he'd looked at her, no disgust or abhorrence about how ugly her arm was. Not like the way it had been with Craig.

Dared she take the risk and let herself believe that?

Maybe if Marco didn't want children of his own, this could work out, because then the effects of NF2 on her pregnancy wouldn't be an issue, the way they had been for Craig.

She knew she was rostered on to Cubicles again for the first part of her shift; so was Marco, and her pulse beat just a little faster at the thought. But when she walked into the staffroom and he greeted her with a casual, 'Hi', the butterflies all sank again. She'd expected a little more warmth to his smile. So did this mean he'd spent the rest of yesterday evening looking up NF2 on the internet and now he felt the same way as her ex-husband—that she had nothing to offer him, no future except unwanted complications?

But she did her best to keep a professional smile on her face and treat Marco just the same as the rest of her colleagues. No way was she going to let anyone realise what an idiot she'd been.

Marco glanced at her. 'We'd better go and do the handover in Cubicles, Sydney.'

'Sure.'

As soon as they were out of earshot of the others, he said, softly, 'Can I see you tonight after our shift, *tesoro*?'

She was about to make a slightly sharp retort when she looked into his eyes. They held the extra heat that had been missing in the staffroom, and then she realised that she was letting her past get in the way. She'd assumed that Marco's reactions would be just the same as Craig's. That he'd back off because she wasn't perfect. But Marco wasn't Craig. She'd just been completely unfair to him, judging him by someone else's standards.

'Everything OK?' he asked.

'Yes. Sorry. Wool-gathering. Yes, I'd like that.'

'Good.' And the expression in his eyes was everything she could have wished for.

She dealt with her first case; her patient had tripped on the kerb on the way to work. Her ankle had hurt slightly at the time, and she'd thought she'd just twisted it, but by lunchtime she'd hardly been able to put weight on it.

'I think it's a sprain,' she said when she'd finished examining the ankle, 'but because you can't put weight on your ankle I'm going to send you for an X-ray to make sure there isn't a tiny fracture.'

While she was waiting for the X-ray results to come through, she headed back to Reception to collect her next patient; on the way, she overheard a deep voice saying, 'Wow, you were a very brave girl. Does it hurt now?'

A slightly wobbly childish voice confided, 'It's a bit sore.'

'OK, sweetheart, I can do something about that, but first I need you to make a fist for me.'

Clearly there was some damage to the little girl's hand, Sydney thought, and Marco was checking for nerve damage.

'That's great. Well done. Can I ask you to help me a bit more?'

'Ye-es.'

'There's this song, but I can't remember the words and I need your help.'

A moment later, a beautiful tenor voice began singing 'Old MacDonald Had a Farm'.

So he was using his distraction technique again, was he? Sydney couldn't help smiling. And she was slightly disappointed to discover that he'd finished singing when she called her first patient back again to put an elastic bandage on her ankle and give her advice about resting her ankle and doing gentle physio exercises.

The shift flew by; but finally she handed over to the night shift. Marco was waiting for her by the restroom. 'I heard you singing, earlier,' she said.

'Ah, to the little girl who'd been bitten by a dog. The wound was infected, so I had to clean it and give her a tetanus shot, as well as antibiotics. I thought it might be wise to start the distraction technique early.'

Marco was excellent at distraction. She knew that, first-hand. 'So did it work?'

He smiled back. 'It helped that I had a different song. I was getting a bit bored with my repertoire.'

'"Incey Wincey Spider" is a good one—as long as the child isn't scared of spiders, that is.'

'I don't know that one. You'll have to teach me.' He raised an eyebrow. 'I'm happy to pay your fees in kisses.' He glanced around, then stole a kiss. 'That's on account.'

Sydney swallowed hard. 'I thought you might have read up on things last night and changed your mind.'

She meant it to come out lightly, but the neediness must've shown in her face, because he said softly, 'I read up on things, yes, but nothing's changed. I just didn't think you'd like the hospital grapevine running overtime about you. That's the only reason I didn't kiss you hello. Properly.' He smiled. 'Well, that and the fact that kissing you would shoot my concentration to pieces and we had patients to see.'

'I hadn't even thought about the hospital grapevine.' But she was glad that he had. When her marriage to Craig had collapsed, the news had been round her old department in what felt like seconds, and she'd hated the fact that people were talking about her. Even though she liked her colleagues, she didn't want to be the subject of gossip.

'So how about I cook dinner for us?'

She blinked. 'You cook?'

He laughed. 'Italian men are very good at three things. Singing, cooking, and...' He drew nearer and whispered in her ear, 'Making love.'

She felt the colour flood into her face and heat coiled

deep in her belly. Was that what he was planning to-night? Making love with her? Anticipation, excitement and fear mingled, sending a shiver down her spine. And they grew stronger as they headed back to his flat.

'Um—can we stop off at the shops so I can buy some wine?' she asked.

'There's no need, *tesoro*. I have wine.'

She coughed. 'Someone insisted on seeing me home last night because that was the way he was brought up. And I was brought up to take flowers, chocolates or wine as a gift if someone's cooking dinner for me.'

'Fair point.' He smiled at her. 'But I'd still rather not stop. If it makes you feel better, maybe you can cook me dinner some time.'

He clearly wasn't going to budge, so there was no point in making a fuss about it. 'OK,' she said, keeping her tone as casual as his.

'Good.'

He led her up the steps to his front door and unlocked it, then ushered her inside and shed his suit jacket. 'Come and sit in the kitchen with me and have a glass of wine. It won't take long to make dinner.' He paused. 'Before I start—are you vegetarian?'

'No. I like most foods—with the exception of Brussels sprouts.' She grimaced. 'My mum always insists that we eat three with our Christmas lunch, be-cause it's traditional.'

He laughed. 'That sounds like a challenge. And I bet I can serve you sprouts and you'd enjoy them.'

'And the stakes are?'

His eyes glittered, and her heart missed a beat. She'd just offered him a challenge. And she was pretty sure that his answer was going to involve sex.

He bent to nuzzle her ear. 'Loser...'

Her mouth went dry, and she could barely breathe.

'...makes pudding.'

Now, that she hadn't expected. And she didn't know whether to laugh, be embarrassed or kiss him, he'd tipped her so completely off balance.

He gestured to the chair next to the small bistro table in his kitchen. 'So, can I pour you some wine? Red or white?'

'I don't mind—whatever goes best with the meal.'

'White,' he said, and took a bottle from the fridge. He poured them both a glass, then lifted his own in a toast. 'To us.'

'To us,' she mumbled, her stomach in knots. A man like Marco Ranieri must be used to dating gorgeous women. She was flawed. Would she live up to his expectations?

'Of course you will.'

Sydney was horrified. 'Oh, no. Please tell me I didn't say that out loud.'

'You did.' He leaned down to kiss her lightly. 'And I'm glad you did, because now I know what's worrying you. Yes, I've dated gorgeous women. And you happen to be gorgeous, so there's no change there.' He lifted a hand to forestall her protest. 'And, yes, I know you have some nodules on one tiny patch of skin.'

Tiny? It was huge, the reason she couldn't even wear a short-sleeved T-shirt.

'I'm not that shallow, *tesoro*,' he said softly. 'I'm interested in the whole package. And I might point out that the ancient Persian rug-makers always wove a flaw into every rug, because nothing is ever perfect.'

She blew out a breath. 'Sorry. That was *really* wet of me.'

He looked thoughtful. 'No. In your shoes, I think I'd find it hard to trust. And you have no idea how good it makes me feel that you're taking a chance on me.' He smiled. 'And now I'm going to feed you.'

'Can I give you a hand with anything?'

'No, you're fine. Just chat to me.'

Sydney thoroughly enjoyed watching Marco cook; he was deft and efficient. Not to mention very easy on the eyes, particularly when he got rid of his tie, undid his top button and rolled his sleeves up. In a suit at work, he was gorgeous; but, here and now, slightly more dishevelled, he looked touchable. Mouthwateringly so.

And dinner was far better than she'd expected: a perfectly presented *tricolore* salad, pasta with pesto, chicken *parmigiana* with steamed green vegetables, and then strawberries and the nicest ice cream Sydney had ever tasted. 'That was fantastic,' she said. 'And you must let me do the washing up.'

'No chance,' he said with a smile.

'Territorial about your kitchen, are you?'

'No. I can think of better uses of our time.'

Her heart skipped a beat at the heat in his eyes.

He made coffee—using a proper espresso machine, she noticed with amusement—and then ushered her through to his living room. She noticed the state-of-the-art TV, music system and games console dominating the room; but there were also full bookshelves, and a guitar propped against one wall.

'Do you play classical or pop?' she asked, indicating the guitar.

'Both. My parents made me have music lessons at

school. I moaned at the time, but I'm glad they did. It's a good way of getting rid of stress.'

'Would you play something for me?'

'Later, sure.'

There were photographs on the mantelpiece; she gestured towards them. 'Can I be nosey?'

'Of course.'

She set her coffee on the low table and took a closer look at the photographs.

'Your parents, your brother and sister?' she guessed, seeing the family resemblance immediately.

'Yes. My brother, Roberto, and my sister, Vittoria. Roberto's the one who runs the business side of things, and Vittoria's the designer—she's incredibly talented.' He came to stand behind her and wrapped one arm round her waist, drawing her back against his body. 'That was taken last summer, in my parents' garden at Capri.'

Overlooking the sea. 'I don't think I've ever seen a sea so blue,' she said.

'Capri's something else,' he agreed. 'I trained in Rome, and I stayed there when I qualified because there were good opportunities there, but I always think of Capri as home. It's where I grew up.' With his free hand, he gently replaced the photograph on the mantelpiece, then turned her to face him. 'Sydney. I know I'm rushing things, but I've been dying to do this all evening and I don't think I can wait any more.'

He kissed her, his mouth sweet and soft and coaxing as it moved against hers; and then, when he deepened the kiss, it felt as if stars were exploding in her head.

Sydney had no idea when or how he'd manoeuvred them over to the sofa, but the next thing she knew she was sitting on his lap, her hands were thrust through his hair, and he'd slid his hands under the hem of her long-sleeved T-shirt and was stroking her abdomen. The more he touched her, the more she wanted him to touch her. And she really, really wanted to touch him. She untucked his shirt from his trousers and began to explore his skin. It was so soft under her fingertips, and yet his body was lean and muscular; clearly he looked after himself. She felt him unsnap her bra, and then he rolled so that she was lying on the sofa and he was kneeling between her thighs.

'You feel gorgeous,' he said as he nuzzled her abdomen. He gradually kissed his way higher; she slid her hands back into his hair and urged him on as his mouth found one nipple. It had been so long, so long since someone had touched her like this, made her feel so amazing...

And then she became aware that he was lifting her slightly so he could take her T-shirt off.

Meaning her arm would be bare, in full view.

She waited for him to recoil. Except he didn't. He kissed her lightly. 'I'm sorry, *tesoro*, I'm rushing you. I'll stop.'

'Yes. No.' She grimaced. 'Sorry, I'm a mess—I'm not used to feeling this way.' She stroked his face with a shaking hand. 'And you're so perfect.'

Perfect? If only she knew the truth about him, Marco thought. But, if she did, he knew she'd put the barriers straight up between them again. And he wouldn't blame her. She'd had a rough time over the past few years and she needed a man she could rely on. He was far from being Dr Reliable—he'd let his wife down in the worst possible way. And how did he know that he wouldn't let Sydney down, the way he'd let Sienna down?

'Nobody's perfect,' he said lightly. 'Certainly not me.'

'Marco, I...' She swallowed hard. 'I do want you. I do want this. But...'

He knew what she wasn't saying. That she felt self-conscious. Awkward. Embarrassed.

'I might just have a solution. And it's because I want you to relax with me, not because I have issues about your skin or your NF2—just so you're clear on that, I don't have any issues at all.' Except commitment issues. Been there, got it badly wrong, and never wanted anyone to pay that kind of price again. But keeping this relationship light and fun didn't mean he could just be selfish and ignore Sydney's needs.

He sat up, finished unbuttoning his shirt and took it off. 'How about I close my eyes while you take your top off and put this on?'

Colour slashed over her cheekbones. 'I'm sorry. I'm being ridiculous.'

'No, you're tense. And I want you to feel amazing, not worried.' He stole a kiss. 'One thing, *tesoro*. Leave the shirt unbuttoned. That way, your arm's covered so you don't feel awkward, but I still get the pleasure of seeing you.'

He'd lied about not being perfect, Sydney thought. Because he'd come up with the best possible solution to her worries. And she really, really appreciated his sensitivity. 'Thank you.'

'Tell me when I can look,' he said softly, and the heat in his gaze sent a thrill down her spine.

Swiftly, she stripped off her T-shirt and bra, then slid his shirt on, like a jacket. It still held the warmth of his body, and she could smell his clean, masculine scent. It felt like being held, being treasured, and tears pricked her eyelids.

'OK,' she whispered.

He opened his eyes and sucked in a breath. 'Wow. Do you have any idea how incredible you…?' He made an impatient gesture with his hand. 'Oh, forget talking.' He pulled her into his arms, kissed her hard, then scooped her up and carried her to his bed.

Sydney was aware of deep, soft pillows and cool, smooth sheets against her skin; but as soon as Marco touched her again the world telescoped down to just the two of them.

She shivered as he undid her jeans and stroked her midriff. He nuzzled his way up to her breasts, and teased her nipples with the tip of his tongue. 'You're gorgeous,' he said. His voice was just that little bit deeper and huskier, telling her that he was as turned on as she was.

Gently, he eased her hips off the bed so he could draw the denim down over her hips. He stroked every centimetre of skin he uncovered and followed it up with kisses as he pulled her jeans down over her thighs, past her knees, over her calves—then started at the hollows of her ankle-bones and kissed his way upwards again.

By the time she felt his mouth grazing her inner thighs, she was quivering. Desperate. It had been years and years since she'd felt like this, a burning need that couldn't be quenched. 'Marco? I need you now,' she whispered. 'Before I implode.'

He stripped in seconds, and retrieved a condom from

his wallet. And then he knelt between her thighs. 'Are you absolutely sure about this, *tesoro*?' he asked.

In answer, she reached up and kissed him.

Slowly, slowly he eased inside her.

She'd forgotten how good this could be—and Marco was more than good. Every touch, every kiss, every caress stoked her desire until she felt as if she couldn't hold on any more. She didn't make a single protest when he gently took his shirt off her, meaning they were completely skin to skin—because that lumpy patch on her arm didn't matter any more. Her legs were wrapped round his waist, he was kissing her, and then her climax hit and everything felt as if it had just gone up in flames. She cried out his name; in answer, his mouth jammed over hers, and she felt his body shuddering against her as he reached his own climax.

He was still holding her when she finally floated back to earth.

'Let me go and deal with this. I'll be back in a second.' He kissed her lightly.

She leaned back against the pillows, hardly able to credit what had just happened. They'd just made love, and he'd kissed her and touched her all over. There was no need for her to feel shy with him. He accepted her for who she was. What she was. Flaws and all. And that was what made the tears so hard to hold back: it had been so, so long since she'd felt this way. Years.

Marco returned to the bedroom, naked and looking completely comfortable in his skin. He took one look at her, sighed, and slid into bed beside her. 'Come here.'

When he pulled her into his arms for a cuddle and stroked her hair, the sweetness of the gesture made her crack. She tried really hard to blink the tears back, but they escaped anyway, dripping onto his skin.

'What's wrong, Sydney?' he asked softly.

How could she explain it? He'd made her feel attractive for the first time in years, and she was finding it overwhelming.

'Did I hurt you?' he asked, looking concerned.

'No.' He'd been gentle. Protective. He'd made her feel amazing. 'I'm just being pathetic.' She dragged in a breath. 'Sorry. It's just…it's been a long time since anyone made me feel this good.'

'If it helps,' he said softly, 'it's the same for me.'

Why would a man like Marco have been single for years? she wondered. He was good company, he was kind, he was more than easy on the eyes—any woman would consider herself lucky if he was hers. 'How come?' The words were out before she could stop them; she bit her lip. 'Sorry. That's prying.'

'It's OK.'

No, it wasn't. She could feel the tension radiating through him. She shifted so that she could stroke his face. 'I'm sorry for bringing back bad memories. Break-ups can be hard.'

'It wasn't a break-up.' A muscle worked in his jaw.

The pain in his eyes made the connection for her. Single, but not because of a break-up; that had to mean something much more final. Her heart contracted sharply. Obviously they'd been happy, and the bottom had dropped out of his world when his partner had died. 'She must've been very special.'

'She was.'

'I won't push,' she said softly, 'but if you ever want someone to listen, I'm here.'

'Thank you.' But none of the tension in his body was gone. If anything, it was worse. He pulled away. 'I'll make us some coffee. The bathroom's next door. Help yourself to what you need. I'll be in the kitchen when you're ready.' He pulled on his jeans, then practically fled from the room.

Oh, hell. She hadn't meant to trample all over his feelings and bring bad memories back for him. She'd shower, then she'd apologise.

Once she'd showered and dressed, she restored order to the crumpled bedclothes, then joined him in the kitchen. 'Sor—' she began, but he shook his head.

'It's fine. I'm sorry. I find it…' he paused and spread his hands in an eloquent gesture '…hard to talk about what happened. But I guess I owe you the facts.'

'You don't owe me anything,' she said softly.

'My wife was killed in an accident, two years ago.' His expression was bleak.

What did you say to someone in the face of such devastation and unexpected loss? She didn't have a clue, but silence would definitely be the wrong thing. All the words she could think of were inadequate—but they would have to do. 'I'm sorry. That's tough, losing someone so young.'

He shrugged. 'Tough things happen to everyone. You just have to deal with them.'

She had the strongest feeling that he hadn't really dealt with it. That coming to London had been an attempt to block out the memories and he still hadn't come to terms with his loss.

He poured her a coffee and added milk. 'Is this OK? Not too strong?'

Clearly he didn't want to talk about it any more. Sure. She'd respect his boundaries. 'It looks fine. Thank you.'

'Good.' He paused. 'So you've lived in London since you joined the London Victoria?'

'Since I was eighteen. I trained in London.'

'So you know the place well.' His smile was slightly forced. 'While I'm here, I'd like to see London properly, and the best way to do that is with someone who knows it. I was wondering if you'd like to be my tour guide, maybe.'

Whether he meant as just a friend, or whether they were still going to see where this thing between them was going, she wasn't sure. But she kept her tone light. 'Sounds like fun. Though where I take you depends on what you like. Museums, theatres, parks...'

'The lot. Definitely the London Eye at night,' he said. 'And all the scientific museums.'

'It's years since I visited them. I'm probably not going to be much cop as a tourist guide,' she warned.

'Then we can explore together. And it'll be even more fun, because it'll be new to both of us,' he said. 'We can make a list and tick things off. Places you've always wanted to see, too, but never got round to visiting.'

Making new memories together, to replace the old bad ones. That definitely sounded good to her, whether he was offering simply friendship or something more. 'That,' she said, lifting her coffee cup, 'is a deal.'

CHAPTER FIVE

By the weekend, Marco and Sydney had worked up a wish-list of places to visit between them; and she realised that she'd forgotten how much fun it was to plan a day out with someone.

She was working an early shift on Saturday while Marco was off duty, so he met her from the hospital after her shift.

'How was your day?' he asked.

'Full of Saturday morning DIY accidents. Hammered thumbs, slipped chisels, and one guy who'll take the five seconds to put on a pair of safety goggles next time he drills something, because it'll save him a trip to hospital and a wait in Reception until we can irrigate his eye to get the tiny bit of plaster out, and then eye drops while we check his scratched retina.' She raised an eyebrow. 'Not to mention the eyepatch and antibiotic drops for the next three days.'

'Ouch. You've just reminded me why I always pay someone to do things like that for me.'

She laughed. 'You must be the first man I know who's admitted to not being able to do DIY.'

'Life's too short to be pompous—and I'd rather spend

my free time doing something I enjoy,' he said with a grin. 'Are we still on for Kew Gardens?'

'We certainly are.'

It didn't take long to get there on the tube and Sydney enjoyed strolling hand in hand through the gardens with Marco.

'It's very pretty,' he said.

'I love this time of year, when the spring flowers are out.' She gestured to the blue carpet of the 'glory of the snow'. 'And these are my absolute favourite.'

'Very English,' he said.

She laughed. 'Maybe you're thinking of the bluebells, and they're at their best at the end of next month—and I'm so going to take you to see English woodland.'

He stooped to whisper in her ear, 'As long as I get a kiss under every tree.'

A thrill went down her spine at his words. She still couldn't quite believe that he enjoyed kissing her—but the glitter in his eyes convinced her. As did the lightest, sweetest, most teasing brush of his lips against hers. 'That's on account.'

The thought of how he'd kiss her later, in private, turned her knees weak.

'So spring's your favourite season?' he asked.

'It's a tie between that and autumn—I love crunching through the fallen leaves on a frosty day.'

'And that would be what, October time? I'm adding that to our list,' he said.

'How about you—what's your favourite?'

'Early summer,' he said, 'when all you can smell in my part of Italy is blossom from the lemon and orange groves.'

'It sounds beautiful.'

'It is. There's nowhere else in the world where I'd rather live.'

His voice was full of passion; and yet he was here in London. Trying to get away from his memories, perhaps? 'What made you choose England?'

'The opportunity to expand my knowledge.'

'Did you ever consider doing a stint with Doctors Without Borders?'

He froze. Oh, hell. The worst possible question she could have asked.

Though it wasn't Sydney's fault. He hadn't told her what had actually happened to Sienna. Sydney wasn't the sort to come out with thoughtless comments or trample on people's feelings. Besides, it was an obvious question to ask an emergency specialist who'd talked about wanting to broaden his experience.

Yet he couldn't bring himself to tell her the truth. To drag up all the pain, the loss, the memories he was trying to keep locked away.

'I thought about it,' he said, forcing himself to keep his tone light, 'but it didn't happen.' This was his cue to ask her whether she'd ever thought about working for Doctors Without Borders, he knew—but he wanted to get off the subject as fast as possible. 'So what's your game plan? Registrar, consultant, head of department?'

'Pretty much. Though I'm also tempted by the teaching side. I like the idea of helping to train new doctors, to give them confidence in their skills and teach them how to see their patients as people, not just as conditions that need to be fixed.'

He nodded. 'Fair point. And I think you'd be good at that. You're calm, you're unflappable, and they'll learn a lot of patient skills by shadowing you.'

To his relief, she didn't push it when he changed the subject back to Kew; as they walked through the gardens, hand in hand, his tension began to ease.

When the first spatters of rain hit them, they headed for the café to take shelter.

He glanced through the window at the sky. 'It looks to me as if it's set in for the day. We'll have to see the rest of Kew another time, I think. Unless you don't mind getting drenched?'

She laughed. 'Are you telling me you're fussy about your hair getting wet?' She reached over to ruffle his hair. 'Actually, you look quite cute like that.'

'Like what?'

'Dishevelled.'

He leaned closer and lowered his voice. 'I can think of a very pleasant way of getting dishevelled...but we might get thrown out of the café, so we'll have to take a rain check on that.'

'Ah, but this isn't rain,' she corrected with a grin. 'It's an April shower.'

He caught her hand and raised it to his lips. 'Shower. That's a nice thought, too.'

He wanted to have a shower with her? Her eyes widened. 'Marco, I...'

'Don't worry, *tesoro*,' he said softly. 'I'm not going to push you into doing anything that makes you feel uncomfortable. Although one day, I assure you, I'm going to make love to you in a shower. *Allora*. What's next on our list? We need something indoors.' He took his mobile phone from his pocket and browsed through the notes they'd made together. 'How about the National Gallery?'

'Good idea. That's a really easy journey from here.'

When they reached central London again, it stopped raining for just long enough that Marco could admire the bronze lions in Trafalgar Square, and then they headed for the gallery.

'Let's go and see the Constables first,' Sydney suggested. 'I love the one with the rainbow over Salisbury Cathedral.'

He dutifully admired them, then took her in search of the van Goghs. 'I have to admit, the Constables were pretty enough, but I prefer these,' he said. '"The Sunflowers" is one of my favourites; it's really good to see the real thing instead of a print.'

She smiled at him. 'I half expected you to be waxing lyrical over the Italian painters.'

He laughed. 'It's not the nationality of the painter that matters; it's whether the painting speaks to me.' How long had it been since he'd visited an art gallery? Or maybe it was more that you never really explored the city where you lived unless you were showing someone around. He and Sienna had been wrapped up in their work and in each other. With Sydney, it was different. And he was enjoying being carefree for once, just having fun and keeping things light.

They wandered round until closing time, stopping here and there to admire a particular painting, then headed back to her flat. It was Marco's turn to wait in the kitchen, sipping a glass of wine, while she made dinner; he was surprised by how much he enjoyed the domesticity. And how much he'd missed it.

'I should've asked you to bring your guitar,' Sydney said. 'It would've been nice to hear you play while I'm cooking.'

'Next time we're at my place, I'll play for you,' he promised.

The food was excellent, but best of all was the pudding.

'I was expecting today to be a bit summery,' Sydney said as she opened the fridge door, 'so I'm afraid this doesn't quite suit the weather. I made it this morning before my shift, though I really should've made you a traditional English pudding—apple crumble and custard or something.'

'This looks nice,' he said as she placed the bowl on the table. 'Trifle?' The top looked like fresh cream, decorated with strawberries.

'Sort of.' She gave him a seriously cheeky smile. 'It's an English twist on a classic Italian pudding. I know strictly it's not tiramisu unless there's coffee in it, but it's the same principle.'

'So what's in it?'

Her eyes sparkled with mischief. 'Guess. If you get it wrong, you have to pay a forfeit.'

'Oh, yes? And if I get it right?'

'Then you choose the forfeit.'

He grinned. 'Sydney Collins, I like the way your mind works.'

She spooned some of it into a bowl for him, and he tasted it. 'Very nice. There's definitely a real vanilla pod, cream and mascarpone. But I can't quite work out what you've soaked the sponge fingers in. Orange juice? White wine?'

'Orange juice, yes; wine, no. So you owe me a forfeit,' she said, looking pleased.

He stood up, caught her round the waist and kissed her lingeringly. 'Will that do?'

'Very nicely.'

He was pleased to see that her cheeks were pink and she was slightly breathless. 'So what's the missing ingredient?'

'Raspberry liqueur.'

'It's a very nice combination.' He finished his dessert. 'Can I be greedy?'

'Help yourself.'

'The problem is, I want you as well.' He scooped her onto his lap and kissed her. 'Though there is a solution.'

'Which is?'

'I take you to bed. And then, afterwards, we eat the rest of the tiramisu.' He paused. 'In bed.'

'That's so decadent.' But she was smiling. 'I like the way your mind works, too, Dr Ranieri.'

'Take me to bed, Sydney,' he said huskily.

She slid off his lap, took his hand and led him to her bedroom. It was a gorgeous room with duck-egg-blue walls, teal curtains and matching bed-linen; the pile of silky cushions on her double bed was covered in a peacock-feather design—strong and vibrant, much like Sydney herself, he thought appreciatively.

She closed the curtains and put the bedside lamp on low. This time, to his pleasure, she let him undress her, though he noticed that she flinched when he took off her long-sleeved T-shirt and bared her arm. To reassure her, he kissed the lumpy patch of skin, then drew her close. 'That wasn't pity, by the way. Like I said, it's the whole package I'm interested in. I like who you are, Sydney, and I like the way you look. I like the way you taste. And I really like the way you feel.'

He skimmed the flat of his palms down her sides, moulding her curves. 'You turn me on in a big way,' he said. He picked her up and laid her on the bed, then tipped her back against the pillows and kissed his way down her body. He loved the fact that he could make this bright, sweet woman wriggle beneath him and make her eyes go hot with desire.

He put on a condom to protect her, then covered her body with his. He couldn't remember the last time it had felt this *right*, the way it did with Sydney. She wrapped her legs round his waist, and he pushed in deeper. She gave a little sigh of pleasure and tipped her head even further back, offering her throat to him. He couldn't resist drawing a path of hot, open-mouthed kisses down her soft, sweet skin. She drew him closer still; Marco could feel the change in her breathing and knew that she was close to climax.

Well, he wasn't ready yet—and he wanted to really blow her mind.

So he slowed everything down. He withdrew slowly, until he was almost out of her, then eased back in, pushing deep, putting just enough pressure on her clitoris to make her gasp.

'Marco—you're driving me insane— I need…' Her breath hitched.

'Open your eyes,' he said softly. 'Look at me.'

She did, and he quickened his pace again. He could see the exact moment that she climaxed and let himself fall over the edge with her.

Afterwards, she lay curled against him.

'Want me to go and get the tiramisu?' he asked.

'No, I'll do it.' She climbed off the bed and belted a silky dressing gown round herself. He half expected her to leave it on when she returned with the bowl and two spoons—but, to his pleasure, she simply handed him the bowl and took off the dressing gown. Without flinching. The fact that she was starting to trust him really warmed him.

Though quite how he was going to get himself to trust her enough to tell her the truth about Sienna's accident, he wasn't sure. He didn't want to see the disappointment in her eyes when he told her just how badly he'd let his wife down—and then make the connection that he'd end up letting her down, too. No, he'd wait. Let himself enjoy this just for a little while longer. And then he'd find the right words.

CHAPTER SIX

OVER the next few days, as well as being in tune with each other outside work, Marco found that he was perfectly in tune with Sydney at work, too. She had good instincts and wasn't afraid to ask questions to get the full picture; and she was so empathetic that patients warmed to her and opened up to her.

At Wednesday lunchtime, the paramedics brought in a girl with acid burns to her hands. 'This is Jasmine. She has acid burns to her hand and arm. It happened at school.'

'It wasn't an accident. Leona did it on purpose,' the girl said, her voice hard. 'She's jealous of me. She said she'd make sure nobody ever fancied me again because the acid would burn my face and make me ugly.'

'The other girl's coming in a separate ambulance,' the paramedic continued. 'The police want to talk to them, once you've finished treating them.'

'Do you know what kind of acid it was?' Sydney asked.

'Dilute hydrochloric acid, according to the teacher. I checked there wasn't any metallic contamination and the teacher had them both wash their hands under running cold water. We continued irrigating her skin in the ambulance,' the paramedic explained.

'Thanks. We'll take it from here,' Marco said. 'Can you check the other girl, when she comes in?' he asked Sydney.

'Sure.'

'Jasmine, I'm Dr Ranieri,' he said to the girl. 'I'll check you over, then give you some pain relief before I start treating the burn.'

When the other ambulance came in, the paramedic introduced the other girl to Sydney and did the handover.

'Leona, I'm Dr Collins. If you can let me have a look at your hands, then I'll give you some pain relief. Can you tell me, were you wearing anything else when this happened? A jumper or anything?'

Leona shook her head and bit her lip.

'OK.' Sydney looked at the girl's skin. It was reddened and blistered, though clearly it had been irrigated thoroughly. She gave the girl pain relief, then checked the PH value of her skin. 'I'm just making sure that all the acid's off your skin before I treat you,' she said. 'With a burn like this, your skin is at risk of infection, so I'm going to put some antibiotic cream on and a dressing.'

'Thank you,' the girl whispered.

Her face was still pale; maybe it was simply that she knew that she was in severe trouble and was worried about the consequences of what she'd done to the other girl. But something didn't feel quite right. Given that this girl was meant to be the one who was aggressive and made threats, how come she was so quiet now and not brazening it out? And Jasmine, who was meant to be the victim, hadn't seemed frightened or upset. There had been a hardness in her voice, too.

But, more than that, there was something else that raised Sydney's suspicions that all wasn't quite as it seemed.

'You'll need to come back and see us in two days, so we can see how you're healing. I just need to have a quick word with my colleague, and then I'll be back to see you. Will you be OK to stay here?'

Leona nodded.

Swiftly, Sydney walked over to the cubicle where Marco was treating Jasmine. 'Can I have a quick word?' she asked.

'Sure.' He excused himself to Jasmine.

'Meg, can you keep an eye on Jasmine for us and make sure she doesn't leave the cubicle or anyone else go in, please?' Sydney asked one of the staff nurses, keeping her voice low.

At Meg's nod, she took Marco to the kitchen, where she knew they wouldn't be overheard.

'What's the problem?' he asked.

'There's something not right about this—I don't think Leona threw acid over Jasmine.'

He frowned. 'How do you mean? They both have acid burns.'

She handed him a plastic cup. 'Imagine this was full of liquid and you were going to throw it over me. How would you stand?'

His frown deepened, but he held the beaker as if he were about to throw the contents over her.

'Now, I can see what you're going to do, or maybe you've told me that you're going to throw that in my face and it's acid—so I put my hands up to protect myself, like this.' She demonstrated holding her arms up to protect herself, with her inner arms facing towards him. 'And if I try to knock the beaker out of your hand, to stop you throwing the contents over me…' She lowered her hands and traced her fingertips over the top of his hand at base of his thumb. 'It's going to spill here, and along here.' She traced further, along the side of his arm.

'That's where my patient's injuries are,' Marco said quietly. 'And if you put your hands up like that to protect yourself, some of it's going to splash over your inner forearm.'

'Which is where my patient's injuries are,' Sydney confirmed.

'So the story we've got is completely the wrong way round. Why's Jasmine claiming it was Leona—and, more to the point, why's Leona taking the blame for it?' Marco asked.

'That's what I can't work out. But I wanted to run my theory by you before I talked to her,' Sydney said.

'I agree with you. Go and see what you can find out from her, and I'll have a quiet word with the police, tell them what we think.' Marco blew out a breath. 'What a mess. Poor kid. She's the one who gets hurt and then the blame's lumped on her as well. My guess is, it's bullying that went further than either of them expected, and now neither of them knows what to do.'

Sydney returned to the cubicle. Leona's face filled with fear as the curtain twitched back, and relaxed again when she recognised the doctor who'd treated her.

'Are you OK?' Sydney asked gently.

Leona nodded.

Sydney sat next to the girl on the bed. 'We need to

talk. I know you didn't throw the acid over Jasmine,' she said softly. 'She might be claiming that you did it, but I know you didn't. So what's the real story?'

Leona remained silent, her face white.

'If someone said they were going to throw acid in my face,' Sydney said, 'I'd put my hands up to protect myself. And maybe I'd try to knock the beaker out of her hands. And if that happened, my injuries would be exactly where yours were. If I tried to throw the acid over someone, and they defended themselves, my injuries would be exactly where Jasmine's are. That's what I wanted to discuss with my colleague, and he agrees with me.'

Hope flared in Leona's eyes, and just as quickly died again. 'It's no use. They'll all back her up and say I did it.'

'Who will?' Sydney asked gently.

'Everyone in the class.' Leona dragged in a breath. 'Jasmine's the most popular girl in our year. Nobody's going to take my word over hers.'

'I do,' Sydney said. 'So does Dr Ranieri. And he's telling the police what we think, right now. When they investigate something, they take account of physical evidence as well as verbal.'

Leona shook her head. 'Who are you going to believe? She's rich and she's pretty and she fits in.'

'She said you were jealous of her,' Sydney said thoughtfully.

Leona swallowed. 'She said she was going to throw acid in my face so I'd be covered in scars and even uglier, and then Sean wouldn't talk to me any more.'

'Is Sean your boyfriend?'

'No, he's hers. He was only talking to me, that's all.

He likes the same music that I do. We were talking about the new single by our favourite band. Of *course* he wouldn't fancy someone like me. I'm not pretty enough.'

I'm not pretty enough. The words echoed in Sydney's head. Exactly how Craig had made her feel, because of the lumpy skin on her arm and the scar on her back. Ugly. And it wasn't just the physical appearance—it was what it stood for. The fact that she was abnormal, a woman with nothing to offer.

Though Marco was teaching her to see things a different way.

'Everyone's got different ideas of what's pretty and what's not,' she said softly. 'And sometimes if people tell us we're ugly, we believe them when it isn't true.'

'I'm not trendy like Jasmine. Mum can't afford to buy me fashionable stuff.'

'And, when you're a teenager, that's tough.' Sydney could still remember the awkwardness of those years. 'But as you grow older, trust me, things change. People see you for who you are, not what you wear. Real beauty isn't about looks, it's about who you are and how you treat others.' She paused. 'You're not ugly, Leona. Far from it. And you don't have to put up with anyone who tells you that. That's bullying, and it's wrong.'

'Who's going to stop her? Last time I told, school didn't believe me. She got one of her friends to lie and say I was trying to get her into trouble. The teacher said it was her word against mine and we should both stop being so silly.'

'But she carried on being nasty to you?'

Leona didn't answer, but Sydney could see the pain in the girl's eyes. No doubt she'd had to put up with plenty of spiteful comments and name-calling.

'Something to think about,' she said softly. 'When a bully's feeling weak, they pick on someone else to make them upset.' Which was exactly what Craig had done with her, blaming her for the end of their marriage. Maybe he hadn't intended to bully her, but he'd felt weak and helpless, and the only way round it for him had been to make her feel guilty for something she had no control over. 'And if they're successful in upsetting someone, it makes them feel powerful, so they keep doing it. If you stand up to the bully, they lose their power.'

'I did stand up to her. And look what happened.' A tear trickled down Leona's face. 'I can't go back to school. Not after this.' Her breath hitched. 'And my mum's going to kill me.'

'Your mum,' Sydney said, 'will be horrified that someone's tried to hurt you.' She put her arm round the girl's shoulders. 'I promise, we'll get all the problems stopped. Remember, you're not the one who started this. It's not your fault, and you're not going to be in trouble for something you didn't do.'

In reply, Leona burst into noisy tears, which Sydney guessed were of relief. She drew the girl closer and held her until the sobs subsided.

'Thank you,' Leona whispered. 'I didn't think anyone would believe me.'

'I do. And we're going to get this sorted out.' Sydney patted her shoulder.

The curtain twitched back, and a woman who looked like an older version of Leona came in, looking terrified. 'Leo! Oh, thank God you're not badly hurt.' She wrapped her arms round her daughter.

'I'll leave you together,' Sydney said. 'The police

are waiting to talk to you whenever you're ready. If you need anything, just ask for me or Dr Ranieri.'

At the end of their shift, Marco and Sydney were both drained.

'That poor girl,' Sydney said. 'Jasmine's been picking on her for years. Her mum had no idea and feels so guilty, poor woman.'

'But she knows now, and the school can do something to stop Jasmine's behaviour,' Marco said. 'Especially now the police are involved. They said it's assault intending to cause grievous bodily harm, so she's in serious trouble.' He raised an eyebrow. 'Just as well for both of them that the acid was more dilute than she thought it was—and that there wasn't any metallic contamination. And the teacher acted fast to irrigate their skin and stop the damage getting worse.'

'It's bad enough—Leona might still be left with scars.' Sydney bit her lip. 'And I was the biggest hypocrite in the world. I told her that beauty's about more than looks.'

'Uh-huh.'

'That's your cue,' she said, 'to say "I told you so".'

'There's no point. You already know it's true.' He took her hand and squeezed it. 'For the record, I think you're beautiful.'

'Thank you.' She squeezed his hand back. 'So are you.'

The following Saturday was bright and sunny, and Marco picked Sydney up in a convertible sports car.

She eyed it. 'You bought this just to use while you're in England?'

He laughed. 'I'm not quite that extravagant. It's a hire car.'

'Which you didn't really need to hire. We could've used my car, you know.'

He wrinkled his nose. 'I'm Italian. I hate being driven.'

'That's got nothing to do with being Italian and everything to do with having a Y chromosome,' she retorted, making him laugh again.

'It's a gorgeous day, *tesoro*. Why would you want to be stuck in a tin can when you can feel the wind in your hair?' he asked, and pushed a button to take the roof down.

'Oh, you show-off,' she teased. Though, to his pleasure, she admitted that the drive to Hampton Court was enormous fun and she was glad he'd hired the car.

'So this is Henry the Eighth's favourite palace,' he said as they walked from the car park and he saw the house for the first time. 'It's a gorgeous building.'

'Garden first, while it's still sunny?' she suggested.

'And the maze. Did you know it's one of the oldest hedge mazes in the world, and it takes twenty minutes to reach the centre?'

She blinked. 'You've been reading up on it?'

'And the house,' he confirmed. 'That way I get the most out of my visit, because I know what I'm looking at and what to look out for. So I also know that we can get to the centre by keeping our right hand on the hedge all the way. It's not the shortest way and we'll still come across dead ends, but we won't get lost.' He smiled. 'And I have plans for the dead ends.'

As in kissing her in every one until she was breathless and her eyes were sparkling.

Once they'd had their fill of the gardens, they headed for the house. Marco shivered as they walked through the long gallery. 'For a warm day, it's really cold in here.'

'Maybe that's because it's supposed to be haunted by Catherine Howard,' Sydney said. 'She was under house arrest and escaped her guards—she ran down here to find the king and plead for her life, but she was caught and dragged back through here to her rooms, screaming all the way.'

'Poor woman.'

'Apparently people tend to feel cold and uncomfortable in the same place,' Sydney mused. 'So maybe you just found the bit she's supposed to haunt.'

'More like it's caused by air currents from the concealed entrances. People know the story, so when they walk into a column of cold air they think it's for supernatural reasons, not scientific.'

'So you don't believe in ghosts?'

'Sometimes,' he said, 'you see what you want to see.' He sighed. 'I guess that's one of the reasons why I left Rome. I kept seeing Sienna, except when I got closer I realised it was just someone who looked a bit like her. Someone who had the same hairstyle or the same body shape or wore the same scarf.'

'I know what you mean. And all the memories in a place, coming back to you when you least expect it and making you wish things could be different. That's why I left my last hospital,' she said. 'I hated seeing the pity in everyone's eyes. Here, they don't know the details—just that I used to be married—and nobody makes a big deal about it.'

'It's a lot easier to cope in a new place without any

memories,' he said. 'You can't change the past. You can't undo what you've done—or do what you've left undone.' It was the nearest he could get to a confession of the truth. For now.

As if she understood, Sydney squeezed his hand. 'All you can do is try to move on. Remember the good stuff and learn to let the bad stuff go.' Her smile was wry. 'Which I guess is easier said than done.'

'I guess we're both trying,' he said. 'Sorry. I didn't mean to make our day full of shadows.'

'I know.' Her fingers tightened briefly round his again. 'Come on. Let's give ourselves a break here and enjoy the rest of the house.'

He forced himself to smile, and by the end of their tour of the house had managed to shake his sombre mood.

When he'd driven them back to London and parked outside Sydney's flat, she said softly, 'I was wondering... We're both off duty tomorrow. Do you want to stay tonight?'

He was tempted. Severely tempted. Waking up with her in his arms, in the morning... But that would be taking their affair up to the next level. He couldn't do it. 'Sorry, I need to get the car back.' He could see in her expression that she was going to suggest following him to the hire-car place in her car and picking him up. 'And then I have some things to sort out back at my flat.' It wasn't true, but it was a kinder way of letting her down. He wasn't rejecting her. He just couldn't do this. The guilt and the fear were too much for him right now.

'Sure.' Her voice was bright and breezy, but he'd caught the glimmer of disappointment in her eyes. He hated himself for it; but he also knew that if she knew the truth about him she'd be even more disappointed. It was better this way.

'I'll see you tomorrow, *tesoro*,' he said. 'If it's dry, we'll go down the river to the Thames Barrier, and if it's wet we'll look at our museums and galleries list.'

'Sure. Goodnight,' she said, and kissed him lightly. 'See you tomorrow.'

He waited until she'd closed her front door behind her, then drove the car back to the hire place. When he let himself into his empty flat, he half wished he'd taken Sydney up on her offer. She was right about needing to move on. And, with her, he was beginning to feel that maybe he could find happiness again.

Yet there was a voice in his head saying, *What if?* What if he let himself get close to her, fell in love with her—what if he lost her, the same way he'd lost Sienna? Could he really face going through all that pain again— the days of numbness, of feeling trapped in a flat, grey world where everything had lost its meaning? Days when he'd forced himself to go through the motions, made himself smile reassuringly at his patients when all the time the grief locked inside him had made him want to howl out the unfairness to the sky.

He'd sworn he'd never let himself get into that position again.

And yet he was drawn to Sydney's warmth. The sparkle in her eyes—a sparkle that he'd put there. He enjoyed her company. And the zing of attraction between them when they made love... Part of him couldn't help thinking that life was short and you should just take happiness where you could find it. He was being given a second chance of happiness—one he didn't really deserve, but he was being given it anyway. So maybe he should grab that chance with both hands.

Maybe.

CHAPTER SEVEN

ON TUESDAY afternoon, Sydney was working in Resus when the paramedics brought in a girl who'd collapsed at her sixth-form college and was confused and disoriented. The girl wasn't up to answering questions, but luckily her best friend had come with her.

'Ruby, what can you tell me about Paige?' Sydney asked.

Ruby bit her lip. 'She's been worrying about being fat. She won't touch anything with carbs in it, because she says carbs make you fatter.' She looked anxious. 'I don't think she's been making herself sick, but she's not eating properly. She's said for ages she's got stomach ache, and I thought it was because she's hungry.'

The girl's breath smelled musty and of pear drops; plus there were definite signs of dehydration. Her pulse was weak, and her heart rate was more rapid than Sydney was happy about.

'Do you have any pain anywhere?' she asked.

'Tummy hurts,' Paige mumbled.

Hunger, some kind of infection, or something else? Sydney wondered. 'OK, I can give you something to help with that. First of all, I'm going to put an oxygen mask on you to help you breathe more easily, and then

I'm going to put some monitors on you to help me diagnose what's wrong.'

Quickly, she put Paige on oxygen and hooked her up to the monitors so she had continuous readouts of her blood pressure and heart rate, as well as her ECG.

There was something else she needed to know, and she thought she might get the true answer from Ruby. 'Sorry, I'm going to have to ask you something awkward,' she said. 'Whatever you tell me stays with me, and you're not going to be in any trouble, but I need to know the truth because it'll affect the treatment I can give Paige. Do you know if she's had any alcohol recently?'

Ruby shook her head.

'Has she been taking any kind of drugs? Something the doctor gave her, or something she bought at the chemist's?' She paused. 'Or even something recreational—as I said, you won't get into trouble, but I need to know the full details so I can give Paige the right treatment.'

'She doesn't do drugs. She doesn't even smoke.'

'That's good. Thank you for being honest with me.' She turned back to Ruby. 'I need to take some blood from you so I can send it to the lab, and I need to do a finger-prick test. You might feel a sharp scratch, but that's all. Is that OK?'

Paige nodded weakly.

Just as Sydney had suspected, the finger-prick test showed high blood glucose levels.

'Ruby, I'll need to ask you to wait outside for a little while so I can do some more tests,' she said. 'Do you know if anyone's managed to get in contact with Paige's parents?'

'Yes, her mum's on her way.'

'That's good. And she's very lucky to have a friend like you.'

'Is she going to be OK?'

Sydney gave her a reassuring smile. 'Yes.'

Ruby looked visibly relieved. 'When she collapsed, I thought…'

Sydney patted her shoulder. 'I know. And it's been tough on you—but you did all the right things. Look, there's a drinks machine round the corner. Go and get yourself a hot chocolate, and then you can come back and see Paige.'

'Thank you.'

'Paige, can you hear me OK?' Sydney asked.

The girl nodded without opening her eyes.

'You're very dehydrated, so I need to put a drip in your arm to give you some fluids. And I'm going to need to put a catheter in so I can measure your fluid input and output and check how your kidneys are doing. Are you a diabetic?'

Paige shook her head.

'Is anyone in your family diabetic?'

Again, a shake of the head.

Once the catheter was in, Sydney was able to test a urine sample; as she'd suspected, it contained ketones and sugar. Was it because, as Ruby said, Paige had been starving herself? Or was it undiagnosed diabetes, brought to crisis point?

She needed a second opinion.

'Dawn, would you mind staying with Paige while I have a quick word with Marco?' she asked.

'Sure,' the staff nurse said.

To her relief, Marco was between patients.

'I need to pick your brains,' she said. 'What do you know about DKA?'

'Diabetic ketoacidosis usually happens when diabetes isn't controlled—and that often happens before it's diagnosed,' Marco said. 'It's more common in younger patients, it's twice as common in women as in men, and it's sometimes brought on by an infection or another illness.'

'I have a patient with what I think is DKA. The glucose levels in her blood and urine are high.' She took him quickly through the case. 'According to her best friend, Paige has been starving herself, so that might have tipped the balance.'

'It's all pointing to DKA, with those glucose and ketone levels.'

'She's dehydrated, so I'm getting fluids into her. Not too fast, because I don't want her to go into cardiac failure or end up with cerebral oedema. I'm planning to add insulin next, then check her potassium levels, and I'm keeping her on a monitor for ECG, heart rate and blood pressure for the time being.'

'Good plan. I take it her parents are coming in?'

'Yes. Her best friend says that her mum's on the way.'

'Do you want me to get in touch with Endocrinology so we can get a diabetes expert down to talk to her mum, and get the ball rolling on a proper diagnosis and treatment for the diabetes?'

'If you don't mind, yes, please—I want to get back and keep monitoring her.'

'Leave it with me. Call me if you need anything else,' Marco said with a smile.

'Thanks.' Sydney returned to her patient, feeling lighter of heart. Marco was utterly reliable and believed in teamwork; she knew he wouldn't forget to do something he'd promised.

Over the next couple of hours, Paige's condition improved, and Sydney was happy to admit her to the endocrinology ward for overnight monitoring. 'The nurses there are very experienced and they'll be happy to answer any questions you have about diabetes,' Sydney told her. 'And, when you're newly diagnosed, of course you'll have questions—they won't think you're being silly. It's their job to make sure you understand your diabetes and how to manage it so you keep well.' She smiled at her. 'And you're lucky you've got a friend like Ruby.'

'She's the best,' Paige whispered. 'I'm so going to buy her chocolates. Except I won't be able to eat any of them with her.'

'That's true, but you can still share other things. You take care now.' She patted Paige's shoulder.

When her shift ended, she went up to see how Paige was doing, and was pleased to see that the girl seemed brighter.

'I forgot to say thank you. For helping me, and being kind,' Paige said. 'And the nurse—sorry, I can't remember her name.'

'Dawn. That's what we're here for,' Sydney said, touched, 'but I'll tell her. I'm glad you're on the mend. The best days of all are when I can do something to help and my patients get better.' She paused. 'Ruby was worrying that you weren't eating properly. You'll need to be careful, in future, because if you don't eat properly you're at risk of your blood sugar going all over the place and making you feel very ill.'

'The dietician's coming to see me tomorrow,' Paige said. 'I don't want to feel like I did this afternoon.'

'So proper eating from now on, yes?'

Paige gave her a wry smile. 'Yes.'

'Good.' Sydney smiled at her. 'I'll let you get some rest.'

When she went back down to the restroom, Marco had already left. But he'd also left a message on her phone: *I'm cooking tonight. Text me when you're on your way M x*

She texted him back. *Leaving now, will bring pudding with me S x*

She called in to a supermarket on the way to his flat and bought a fresh pineapple and some seriously good vanilla ice cream.

Marco met her at the door and kissed her lingeringly. 'Fresh pineapple. What a treat. I take it you went up to see young Paige?'

'Yes. She's on the mend and knows she has to eat properly in future—and thank you for your advice.'

'All I did was confirm what you already knew.' He slid his arms round her and drew her close. 'Ellen says you have the makings of a brilliant registrar, and she's right.'

'I'm not there yet. I still have a bit to learn.'

He kissed her. 'And you're humble with it—one of the things I like about you.'

'Thank you.' She smiled at him. 'So how was your day?'

'OK. It was my day for arm injuries. Sprains, bangs and a dislocated elbow from a toddler who fell over in the supermarket and wouldn't let anyone touch his arm. I ended up going through my whole repertoire of songs before he'd let me put his elbow back in place. I sent him off with a big smile and a shiny sticker.'

'Oh, bless. You're so good with the little ones.' Then her smile faded. What an excellent father Marco would make. But that was yet another reason why this thing between them couldn't be more than temporary; she wouldn't be able to give him children. Not without a lot of risks—and it just wasn't fair to expect him to shoulder those risks.

She forced the thought away and enjoyed her evening with him, curled up on the sofa together watching a film.

'On Friday, you're on an early, yes?' he asked.

'Yes. Why?'

'Because we're going out.' He paused. 'Dress up.'

Dress up. It wasn't something she did very often. Most of the time, when she went out with friends, the dress code was smart casual. Long-sleeved tops and jeans were fine. And it had been ages since she'd been to a wedding or a christening.

She looked through her wardrobe that evening when she got home; there were a couple of long-sleeved dresses, but they were too everyday.

Help.

At least tomorrow was Thursday, late-night shopping evening, so she'd be able to get something—but she wouldn't have time to look in many shops. A quick trawl on the internet found her a gorgeous long-sleeved lace dress, in a retro sixties look with black lace over a contrasting lining. She scribbled down the relevant details, then rang the shop during her break the next morning to see if they had it in her size. Amazingly, they did, and they agreed to put it by for her. After her shift, she sent Marco a text: *Gone shopping for girly stuff, see you tomorrow S x*

When she tried the dress on, she found it was a bit shorter than she'd usually wear, but Marco had been definite when he'd asked her to dress up. And anyway her legs were reasonable, it was just her arm, and the lining of the dress covered that. It was perfect. She had a pair of black patent-leather court shoes that would go brilliantly with it; and it was warm enough in the evenings now that she wouldn't need a coat or even a wrap.

Marco wouldn't even give her a clue where they were going; anticipation and excitement buzzed through her all the next day. He was picking her up at seven, so she dashed home after her shift and took the time to dry her hair properly and put make-up on.

Marco felt his jaw drop as Sydney opened the door to him. 'Wow, you look amazing. I mean, not that you normally don't look nice. But...' He shook his head and smiled. 'Wow.' The high heels and the length of the dress made her legs look as if they went on for ever. And she'd gone for the barely-there kind of make-up that he knew took a lot of effort.

'I scrub up OK, do I?'

'More than OK.' So much so, that he couldn't help yanking her into his arms and kissing her. Thoroughly. He pulled back to smiled at her, then grimaced. 'Sorry, you'll have to redo your lipstick. There isn't a scrap of it left.'

She just laughed, looking pleased.

He glanced at her shoes. 'We won't be walking very far, but are you OK to walk in those?'

She smiled. 'Marco, I'm thirty years old. I know better than to buy shoes I can't walk in.'

'Not necessarily. My sister Vittoria's heading for thirty-five and she buys impossible shoes.'

'She's a dress designer, so she's allowed to. I'm a doctor. I know how good flat shoes are.'

He laughed and kissed her again, then led her to the taxi.

She repaired her lipstick just before the taxi pulled away. 'So where are we going?'

'The London Eye—I've booked us tickets.' Not just tickets, but he was looking forward to seeing her face when she found out.

The taxi dropped them off on the South Bank; they walked across to Jubilee Gardens, where the London Eye was all lit up as dusk started to fall. Marco led her to the fast-track entrance. 'I hate queues.'

The capsule had two champagne cocktails waiting for them.

'Marco? Why are there only two glasses?' she asked, sounding puzzled.

'Because there are only two of us. We have a private capsule.'

She looked shocked. 'This must've cost you a fortune.'

He flapped his hand dismissively. 'Money's not a problem, *tesoro*. And I wanted to enjoy this just with you.'

Her eyes narrowed. 'Oh, no—is it your birthday and I've missed it?'

He stole a kiss. 'No, my birthday's in March—there's no particular reason for this. It's just something I wanted to do and I wanted to share with you. And really don't worry about the money. When my parents retired, they bought me a flat in Rome in lieu of a share of the business, so I'm not exactly poor.'

'Thank you—and now I know why you wanted me to dress up.'

'Absolutely.' Though he hadn't finished, yet.

They watched as London spread out before them, lit up and beautiful. When their capsule reached the very top of the Eye, Marco kissed her; there was a sweetness and an intensity in his kiss that sent a thrill all the way through her. She'd never, ever done anything like this before, and it was just amazing.

'Thank you,' she said when they reached the bottom. 'That was incredible. I feel like a princess, totally spoiled.'

'My pleasure, *tesoro*. I enjoyed it too. And the night isn't over yet—we still have to eat.'

'Dinner's my bill,' she said immediately.

'No.'

'Marco, you paid for the London Eye trip—and it was more than just a normal flight, it was really something special. The least I can do is buy you dinner in return.'

'No. This is my evening, and I want to spoil you. So no arguments, OK?'

Dinner turned out to be in a very swish restaurant in the middle of the city—with a chef whose name she recognised immediately. 'This place has a Michelin star!'

He shrugged. 'And? I like good food.'

'Don't you have to book a table ages in advance?'

'I struck lucky. There was a cancellation.' He smiled at her. 'Now, stop worrying—just enjoy.'

Their table was by a window with an amazing view over London. The food was fabulous, and at the end they shared a tasting plate of the chef's signature puddings. After some of the best coffee and *petits fours* she'd ever tasted, they took a taxi back to her flat.

'That has to be the best evening I've had in years,' she said.

'Me, too,' he said. 'I'll always think of tonight when I think of London.' He touched his mouth to hers. 'London, and you.' He undid the zip at the back of her dress and traced the line of her spine with his fingertips; she shivered, arching her back and tipping her head back so he could kiss the hollows of her throat.

'Turn round,' he said softly, and she did so.

He gently slid her dress off her shoulders, then kissed his way down her spine as he eased the material down over her hips. Her dress fell to the floor and he smoothed his palms down her thighs. 'I want to touch you, Sydney. Taste you.'

He was still on his haunches when he turned her to face him, so his face was level with her navel; he laid his cheek against her abdomen. 'You're so soft and you smell so sweet.' He brushed kisses across her skin, working his way up; she shivered as he straightened up, wanting more.

He traced the lacy edge of her bra and drew one shoulder strap down, and then the other, before kissing his way along her exposed skin. 'So soft, so smooth, so kissable.'

She shivered. 'How come I'm in my underwear and you're still dressed?'

'Because you haven't taken my clothes off yet.' His

dark eyes glittered with pleasure. 'I'm in your hands,' he whispered. 'All yours.'

'All mine,' she repeated. For now. And she was going to make the most of it.

She removed his tie, then undid the buttons of his shirt; she took her time, retaliating for the way he'd undressed her so slowly. She could feel his breath hitch as the pads of her fingertips teased his skin. Good. She wanted him to be as turned on as she was, as desperate for her as she was for him. Finally, she pushed the soft cotton from his shoulders, letting it fall to the floor.

She leaned forward and pressed a hot, open-mouthed kiss against his throat; he arched his head back, giving her better access, and closed his eyes in bliss as she nibbled her way across his skin.

Her hands stroked over his pecs, his abdomen. 'You look like a model from a perfume ad.'

'Is that right?'

'A really, really sexy perfume ad,' she said.

It was enough to snap his control. The next thing she knew, they were both naked, she was in his arms, and he was carrying her through to her bedroom.

He gently laid her on the bed and switched on the lamp.

Then he froze.

'What's wrong?'

'Condom. It's in my wallet. Give me two seconds.'

Yet more proof that Marco wasn't like other men; he knew she was on the Pill, but he also knew that she was adamant about avoiding any risk of pregnancy, so he hadn't complained about her request to use an extra form of protection.

He came back with the little foil packet, and the

desire in his eyes was so strong that it made her catch her breath.

'Sydney.' He kissed her throat, nuzzled the hollows of her collarbones; in turn she was stroking him, touching him, urging him on.

He moved lower, took one nipple into his mouth and sucked. Within seconds, her hands were fisted in his hair and breathing became much, much more difficult. He moved lower, nuzzling her belly, and slid one hand between her thighs; she couldn't help a needy little moan escaping her.

'You feel hot,' he whispered as he cupped her sex. 'Wet.' He skated a fingertip across her clitoris.

'Now, Marco,' she whispered. 'Please now.'

He didn't need her to ask twice; he ripped open the foil packet, rolled the condom on and slid inside her. She wrapped her legs round his waist to draw him deeper.

'You feel amazing,' he whispered.

'So do you.' Her voice sounded shaky.

'OK?'

'Very OK. You send me up in flames.'

He lowered his mouth to hers in a warm, sweet, reassuring kiss.

Pleasure spiralled through her and it was as if he could read her mind; he slowed everything right down, focusing on the pleasure and pushing deeper, deeper. Slow and intense and so incredibly sexy that her climax splintered through her, shocking her by how fast and how deep it was. As her body tightened round his, it pushed him into his own climax; and it was like nothing she'd experienced before, a weird feeling of being at one with the universe.

He stayed where he was, careful not to crush her with

his weight and yet clearly not wanting to move and be apart from her. And it felt like a declaration. Neither of them said a word, but she could see in his eyes that he felt it, too. Things were changing between them. Could they start to believe in the future?

CHAPTER EIGHT

At the team quiz night out at the local pub, the following weekend, Marco ended up sitting next to Sydney. By the end of the evening, his arm was resting casually across the back of her chair.

'So how long have you two been an item?' Dawn asked.

Sydney felt her eyes widen; automatically, she glanced at Marco. How were they going to get out of this without telling a pack of lies?

'Don't deny it. You've both gone red—even you, Marco, the King of Cool,' Dawn teased with a smile.

'We're just good friends,' Marco protested.

Pete laughed. 'Which everyone knows is a euphemism for seeing each other.'

'Looks as if we've just been busted,' Marco said, sounding resigned, and drew Sydney closer.

'We were trying to avoid the hospital grapevine,' Sydney explained.

'*Nobody* can avoid the hospital grapevine,' Pete said. 'At least, not for long. And now we know why you two are so in tune at work.'

'That,' Marco said, 'is because we're both observant.'

'No, it's more than that—half the time you second-guess each other,' Dawn said. 'Pete's right.' She smiled. 'And you're good together.'

'Yeah. She's not bad.' Marco ruffled her hair.

'Neither's he, for a clotheshorse,' Sydney retorted, and everyone laughed.

Afterwards, when everyone was breaking into little groups to travel home together, Marina Fenton caught her arm. 'I'm so pleased for you, Syd. He's a lovely guy, and it's about time you found someone who'll treat you properly.' She paused. 'I take it he knows?'

Sydney knew what she was referring to—Marina was one of the few people who knew about her NF2— and nodded. 'He says it doesn't bother him.'

'Which is just how it should be.' Marina hugged her. 'That's brilliant.'

'Don't start planning wedding bells or anything,' Sydney warned. 'We're just seeing where things take us. Having fun. And I'm fine with that.'

'You don't have to justify yourself to me, Syd,' Marina said. 'As long as you're happy.'

Marco and Sydney walked back to his flat with their arms round each other.

'Are you OK with our colleagues knowing about us?' Marco asked.

'Yes. They're a nice bunch. I don't think they'll give us a hard time.'

'Good.' He let them into his flat. 'Can I get you a glass of wine?'

'Could I be really middle-aged and have hot chocolate?'

He smiled. 'There's nothing middle-aged about chocolate. And you've a way to go anyway before you're middle-aged—I'm not middle-aged, and I'm two years older than you are.' He made a mug of chocolate for her, and coffee for himself.

'So are you going to play something for me?' she asked, gesturing to his guitar, when he ushered her into his living room.

'Sure. What do you want, pop or classical?'

'Classical, I think, please. Something mellow.'

He played her a couple of pieces she recognised.

'Was that Bach?' she asked.

'One of the lute suites,' he confirmed.

'You're really good. Did you ever think about being a musician rather than a doctor?'

He shook his head. 'It's my way of relaxing more than anything else. I wanted to be a doctor from when I was about…oh, twelve or so. I liked the idea of being able to fix things.'

She wasn't surprised; he'd tried to fix her, too. And so far he'd made a pretty good job of it. He'd healed a lot of her scars.

'How about you?' he asked.

'We're not really musical in our family. I sing along with the radio, like most people do, but that's as far as I go.'

'Sing with me?' he asked.

She wrinkled her nose. 'I'm not good enough.'

'We're not making a record,' he said with a smile, 'we're having fun—and anyway, you forget that I've already heard you sing.' He played the beginning of 'Walking on Sunshine'.

She groaned, remembering the way he'd sung her through the abseil. 'Marco, I'm not in the mood for something energetic.'

'Even if I'm not going to make you walk backwards off a tower?' he teased.

'Even if,' she said, smiling.

'OK. Something soft. Do you know this one?' He played the opening of a ballad that had topped the charts a couple of years before.

'I only know the chorus,' she admitted.

'That'll do.' He got her to join in with the chorus, and Sydney was surprised to discover how much she enjoyed it. He segued into another ballad whose chorus she knew. And then he sang another one she didn't know at all, but the lyrics brought tears to her eyes.

'Hey, I didn't mean to make you cry.' Marco propped the guitar back against the wall and then sat beside her on the sofa. He scooped her onto his lap and held her close.

'Sorry, I'm being wet again—but that's such a lovely song. The words are just gorgeous.' All about his girl-friend being amazing, just the way she was—the kind of acceptance she hadn't had from Craig, but Marco could've been singing that song just for her because that was exactly how he treated her. As if she was amazing, perfect, just the way she was.

She stroked his face. 'And your voice is fantastic.'

'Thank you.' He kissed her, his mouth soft and coax-ing, and then he deepened the kiss and she felt desire flooding through her veins. She didn't protest when Marco carried her to his bed.

Later that month, a sickness bug hit the hospital. The departments were all running on a skeleton staff, who all worked crazy hours to try and cover for colleagues who'd been laid low with the bug.

Halfway through Sydney's shift, she knew she'd fallen victim—her head felt hot and any second now...

She excused herself to her patient, bolted for the nearest toilet, and just made it to the sink before she was violently sick.

No way was she going to be able to finish treating her patients. And the last thing she wanted to do was to give a virus to someone on top of whatever medical problem they already had. She splashed her face with water, cleaned up the bathroom and then, taking a kidney bowl with her in case the sickness caught her unawares, went in search of Ellen.

One look at her, and the head of department sighed. 'You've got it, too, Syd?'

'Yes. Sorry.'

'Go home. I'll arrange cover.'

'I've got a patient with an ankle injury in Cubicles. I apologised to him before I dashed out, but—'

'The last thing he needs is for you to fix his ankle and send him home with your bug,' Ellen interrupted gently. 'Go home. I'll sort it and let everyone know where you are. Don't come back until you're fully over it, OK?'

'Thank you,' Sydney said gratefully.

She just about made it back to her flat before she was sick again. The only thing she was fit for was grabbing a bowl to be sick in, a glass of cold water, and falling into bed.

She slept for most of the afternoon, and then she was aware that her entryphone was buzzing.

Clutching the bowl, she staggered towards it. 'Yes?'

'Buzz me in,' Marco said.

'No. I've got the sicky bug.'

'And I have the constitution of an ox—as well as rehydration sachets and paracetamol. Buzz me in.'

She couldn't face arguing, so she did what he asked.

'*Tesoro*, you look terrible,' he said when he walked in the front door, carrying a bag of what looked like groceries and a laptop case. Frowning, he laid his fingers against her forehead. 'And you're burning up. Did you take paracetamol?'

'No.'

'I didn't think you would've done, somehow,' he said dryly. 'Medics are the worst patients. Go back to bed. I'll bring you some through in a moment.'

She could hear him moving around in the kitchen, doors opening and closing and the chink of a glass. A few moments later, he came in with a cool flannel and a glass. He gently wiped her face.

'Thank you,' she whispered. 'That feels better.'

'Good. Now, take these.' He gave her two paracetamol tablets. 'I don't need to tell you why.'

To bring her temperature down. Obediently, she took the tablets.

'And now you need to drink this.'

She took a mouthful and pulled a face. 'That's vile. Oral rehydration solution?'

'Because you've been sick, your electrolytes are out of balance, and you know as well as I do that flat fizzy drinks contain way too much sugar and not enough salt and it doesn't work. This stuff does. Keep taking little sips. *Bene*,' he praised as she did what he asked.

He made sure her pillows were comfortable and settled her again. 'You have a bowl? Good. Back in a moment.'

This time, he brought her cool water with a slice of

lime. 'It'll make your mouth feel a bit nicer,' he said. And he'd brought her a pile of magazines. 'I wasn't sure what you liked, so I got you a selection.' He rested his hand briefly against her cheek. 'But if you don't feel up to reading, just rest. I'm going to cook you something light.'

She shook her head, her stomach already protesting at the thought. 'I'd rather not.'

'I promise, *tesoro*, you'll be able to keep this down. Now rest.'

She leafed through the pile of magazines. He'd meant it when he'd said he'd bought a selection: a celeb magazine; a glossy women's magazine; a satirical magazine; and a scientific journal. And it really touched her that he'd made so much of an effort.

Not feeling quite up to reading, she closed her eyes and rested. A few minutes later, Marco reappeared with a tray.

'Chicken soup. Not home-made, I'm afraid, but it's from the deli round the corner from my flat, which is the next best thing. It's light and it's nourishing.'

'Thank you.' She looked at it. 'Marco, it's so kind of you, but I really don't think I can face it.'

'*Tesoro*, you need to keep your strength up. And this is the perfect thing. Just take one mouthful,' he coaxed.

In the end, she managed half a bowl.

'Rest, now,' he directed. 'I'll bring you a drink in half an hour.'

'Marco, I can't expect you to spend your evening here.'

'I'm staying,' he said. 'Because I want to look after

you. And I have my laptop with me, so don't worry, you're not holding me back from anything.'

She blinked. 'You're staying?' Was he saying what she thought he was saying? Taking their relationship to the next stage? 'Tonight?'

'Mmm-hmm. It means I'll need to leave a little bit early in the morning, so I can change at my place—but I'm staying with you until you're better.' He stroked her hair. 'Now, rest. Call me if you need me.'

He was just doing the decent thing and looking after Sydney while she was ill, Marco told himself as he went into the kitchen and ate his own soup. He'd do the same for any of his colleagues.

He told himself the same thing at three o'clock next morning, when he was wide awake, his body curled protectively round Sydney's—and he knew he was lying to himself. He hadn't spent the whole night with anyone since Sienna; the fact that he was here in Sydney's bed had nothing to do with the fact that she was ill, and everything to do with the fact that now he had an excuse to stay.

Part of him wanted to flee from the intimacy, because this was nothing like the casual, fun fling he'd expected it to be. And yet part of him desperately wanted to stay, rather than go back to the lonely life he'd led for the past couple of years. Here, with Sydney in his arms, it felt so right...

But was he kidding himself? If things came to the crunch, would he end up letting her down the way he'd let Sienna down? Could he trust himself to do the right thing for her?

Right then, he had no answers. But he took comfort

in the warmth of her body next to his, her regular breathing, and finally he fell asleep.

Once Sydney had recovered from the bug—which Marco, true to his predictions, didn't get—things didn't quite go back to normal. Because Marco found himself spending more nights at Sydney's flat than at his own. He didn't move in officially; though he kept a spare toothbrush and razor at her flat, and brought a change of clothes if he was working an early shift, simply to make life easy for them. And occasionally at weekends Sydney stayed at his flat, though again she didn't keep more than a spare toothbrush in his bathroom, or brought a change of clothes with her.

It was still a fling, Marco told himself. And they were still working their way through his list of must-sees in London, including walking Beatles-style over the zebra crossing in Abbey Road and getting a passer-by to take their photograph, visiting the Tower of London to see the ravens, seeing all the fascinating specimens in jars at the Hunterian Museum, and then going to see the oldest operating theatre in Europe, in the roof of St Thomas's church.

'It's stunning to think that two hundred years ago surgeons could do an amputation in less than a minute,' he said. 'And with a huge audience.'

'They didn't have much choice, with no anaesthetic or antiseptic available, and having an audience like this while they worked was the only way they could teach their students. Lucky for our patients that it's not like this now.' Her tone was light, but something in her expression told Marco that he'd just touched on a sensitive subject. Of course. She'd had operations to remove tumours on her spine. Two hundred years ago, she wouldn't have survived the invasive procedure.

He slid his arm round her and held her close. 'OK?' he asked softly.

'I'm fine.' Though she sounded just a little too bright and breezy for his liking.

In the middle of the week, he was surprised when she had breakfast with him in her dressing gown. 'Are you on a late today?' he asked.

'No. Day off. Errands to run,' she said. 'I'll call you later, OK?'

She was being evasive, but Marco didn't push it. 'OK.' He kissed her lightly. 'I have to run or I'll be late for my shift. Have fun doing your errands. Dinner at my place tonight?'

'That'd be lovely. I'll text you if I'm running late.' She smiled. 'You know how it is—queues and waiting.'

'Can't you do whatever it is online?'

'No,' she said, but she didn't elaborate.

He found out why, later that evening, when she arrived at his flat.

'Get all your errands done?' he asked.

'For another year,' she said.

He frowned. 'What do you mean, for another year?'

'It was my annual check-up.'

She'd told him she had errands. Not quite how he would've described medical procedures. 'If you'd said, I would've come with you.'

She flapped a dismissive hand. 'Honestly, there was no need. I'm used to it, and there's an awful lot of waiting around. You wouldn't have been allowed in with me for the scans, in any case.'

'I could still have sat in the waiting room with you, kept you company.'

'It's OK. I had a book with me.'

His curiosity got the better of him. 'So how did you get on?'

'I had a scan of my brain and spine, balance tests and eye exams. Just to see what the changes are from last year, and whether we need to act or keep a watching brief.' She smiled. 'There's no change from last time on the schwannomas on my vestibular nerves. So I'm good to go.'

'Well, I'm glad about that. But I wish you'd told me.'

'It's just routine. Nothing scary.' She kissed him lightly. 'Don't fuss. Can I give you a hand with dinner?'

It amazed him, how brave and matter-of-fact she was about it all. But if he told her how remarkable she was, she'd dismiss it. He contented himself with returning her kiss. 'Sure you can. And we need to plan where we're going this weekend. Didn't you promise me some bluebells?'

She smiled. 'Yes. And I remember you promised me, something, too.'

A kiss underneath every tree. He remembered. 'And I always keep my promises.' Well. Almost always. The one time he hadn't... He pushed the thought away. That had been then. This was now. And he needed to be fair to Sydney.

CHAPTER NINE

Two weeks later, Sydney woke feeling out of sorts. She'd slept badly; maybe she'd grown too used to Marco being there at night, because the bed felt too big without him, and she felt lonely when she woke on her own—which was utterly ridiculous and made her cross with herself for being so daft. Yes, they'd become closer since they'd been outed as a couple at work, and more so since he'd looked after her when she'd had the vomiting bug, but it was still only a fling between them. It would be stupid of her to read anything more into it than that.

But she didn't feel herself all morning.

'Are you all right, Doctor?' one of her patients asked as Sydney examined her injured hand.

'Fine, thanks,' Sydney lied through gritted teeth. She could hardly tell the poor woman that her perfume was so strong that it was making Sydney feel queasy.

'You look a bit pale.'

Because she was trying to keep down the nausea. Oh, don't say the sicky bug had returned. Though she wasn't aware of anyone else going down with it again. 'I'm fine,' she fibbed again, and forced herself to concentrate on suturing the nasty gash.

She was still feeling rough in the afternoon. In the

ladies', she adjusted her bra. Maybe it had shrunk in the wash, or something, but it felt too tight and her breasts were sore. And she was going to have to cut back on the amount of water she was drinking, because these trips to the loo were getting ridiculous.

Her breath caught as she thought about it. Sore breasts, feeling sick, frequent micturition… Then she shook herself. Of course she couldn't be pregnant. She was on the Pill, and she and Marco used condoms as well for extra protection. They'd been very, very careful not to take any risks. Babies weren't on the agenda.

And yet she'd had that sickness bug, which would've affected the Pill. Supposing one of the condoms had been faulty?

No. She dismissed the idea as totally far-fetched. How rare was it that there was a problem with a condom? She was probably just feeling premenstrual, that was all.

But the thought wouldn't go away. Every time she said goodbye to one patient and walked down to Reception to collect the next, the question slid insidiously into the front of her mind. Was she expecting Marco's baby?

She was glad that her shift wasn't the same as Marco's today; she needed a little bit of time to get things straight in her head. Starting with buying a pregnancy test in a supermarket at the end of her shift, so she could prove to herself once and for all that she wasn't pregnant and she was just premenstrual and hormonal and grumpy.

She let herself into her flat, put the box on the kitchen table, and made herself a cup of tea. It tasted absolutely awful. Obviously the milk was out of date and she hadn't noticed, because she'd spent the last two nights at Marco's flat instead of at her own. She poured the cup of tea away, got rid of the milk and then picked up the box. Time to settle things and find out the truth.

The test took only a few seconds. She put cap the on the stick and checked the display: one blue line, so she knew that the test was working. The second blue line gradually appeared, and she sagged in relief. Just as she'd hoped. Not pregnant. Now she could stop worrying and get on with her life.

She washed her hands and was about to put the test in the bin when she noticed something and went cold.

The test result couldn't have changed from negative to positive in the space of a few seconds. It just couldn't have done.

But the lines were very dark and very clear, telling her that the worst thing possible had happened.

She was pregnant.

Bile rose in her throat. What on earth was she going to do?

She *couldn't* have a baby. The odds were way too high that the baby would inherit her neurofibromatosis. One in two. The toss of a coin. How could she gamble with a child's health like that? Worse still, if the baby *was* affected, the geneticists wouldn't be able to tell her how severely the baby would have the condition. And the baby might be much more severely affected than she was herself. How could she condemn her child to a life of struggling with mobility and learning difficulties?

She sank to the bathroom floor and drew her knees up to her chin, wrapping her arms round her legs and resting her chin on her knees. It felt as if the bottom had just dropped out of her world, and she was too numb to cry.

Pregnant.

How would Marco react when she told him? OK, so he'd been brilliant with her when she'd been ill. But a short-lived bug wasn't at all the same thing as a pregnancy with possible complications; and in turn nine months of pregnancy wasn't the same as eighteen years of bringing up a child—with or without a disability. Marco was great with kids at work, but that was all part of his job: it didn't mean that he wanted children of his own. Besides, he was the kind of man who liked Michelin-starred restaurants and open-topped sports cars. That hardly went with the kind of lifestyle involving babies and toddlers, sensible cars and family-friendly restaurants with high chairs.

Though he was also a good man, the sort of man who believed in doing the right thing. If she told him she was expecting his baby, she knew he'd offer to change his plans to go back to Italy and he'd stand by her. But she didn't want him to stay with her out of a sense of duty. It'd be fine, at first, but eventually he'd start thinking of the plans he'd put on ice for her. He'd feel trapped, and he'd start to resent both her and the baby for holding him back.

She spent a miserable evening thinking about what to do next—and, however hard she tried, she just couldn't work out what was the right thing to do. Even writing down the pros and cons didn't help. There seemed to be a mile-long list of cons for every option, balancing out the pros.

When the phone rang, she picked it up without thinking, glad of something to distract her from her thoughts.

'Hi.' Marco's voice was warm, and it felt like a hug;

she had to fight back the tears. 'I've just finished my shift. Have you eaten yet?'

'Yes,' she fibbed. She'd been too upset and miserable to eat. And now she was way past hunger.

'OK. If I bring pizza with me, can I come over?'

The idea of pizza made her feel sick, but she said brightly, 'Sure. See you in a bit.'

'Ciao, tesoro.'

Well, she needed to talk to him about it. It might as well be sooner than later. The longer you put things off, the worse the situation became—whether it was a rusty patch on a car, a leaking tap or a medical condition. Better to sort things out as early as possible.

But, when he arrived, she found that all the words had dried up.

And the scent of the pizza made her feel really, really queasy.

'Are you OK?' he asked, looking concerned.

This was it. Her cue to tell him.

Except how did you tell your fun, flirty lover that things had just got a whole lot more serious?

'Just tired,' she mumbled.

'Do you want me to go back to my place?'

Yes. No. Both, at the same time. She couldn't answer.

He frowned. 'Sydney, are you sure you're all right? I know you said your check-up was all clear, but if you've got a tumour that's suddenly decided to grow and started pressing on a nerve and is causing you problems...'

'No.' But that was a real possibility for the future. Pregnancy would affect her condition. The tumours were likely to grow more quickly—and the ones on the vestibular nerves could affect her balance as well as her hearing. She'd be no good at work—she'd keel over all the time. And how unfair would that be on her colleagues? 'I'm just tired,' she fibbed again. *She had to tell him. Now.* But she couldn't find the right words.

'Go to bed, *tesoro*. I'll clear up in here when I've finished, and then I'll join you.'

But she couldn't sleep, even with Marco's arms wrapped round her. She kept plumping her pillow up and shifting to get a more comfortable sleeping position, but it didn't work. She tried willing herself to go to sleep, but that failed, too. Counting sheep was useless.

In the end, not wanting to disturb Marco, she slid out of bed, pulled on her dressing gown, and went to sit in the kitchen. She left the light off so it wouldn't wake him, and sat there in the dark with her elbows propped on the table and her chin resting on her hands.

Pregnant.

With complications.

How was she going to tell him?

She shrieked as the kitchen light snapped on—she'd been so lost in her thoughts and worries that she hadn't heard Marco come in.

'Things obviously aren't OK, *tesoro*, or you wouldn't be sitting here alone in the dark, in the middle of the night.' Marco came to sit beside her. 'You look worried sick. And now I'm worried about you, so will you please tell me what's wrong?'

'I…' A tear leaked out before she could stop it, and she dashed it away.

'Whatever it is, we can sort it out.' He wrapped his arms round her. 'Just tell me.'

She was shaking too hard to talk, trying desperately to keep the tears back.

'Sydney, talk to me. Please.'

She dragged in a breath. 'I don't know how to tell you.'

'You had a letter from your consultant? They made a mistake with the tests?'

'No, nothing like that.'

'Then what, *tesoro*?'

She closed her eyes as she forced the words out, not wanting to look at him and see the horror in his face. 'I'm pregnant.'

Pregnant? Sydney was *pregnant*?

Marco stared at her in utter shock.

She couldn't be.

Given her condition, they'd had to be really careful about contraception. Even though she was on the Pill, they'd used condoms as well, just to be safe. There was practically zero chance of her conceiving.

Except she'd had that sickness bug.

And condoms—rarely—could fail.

And it only took one sperm to fertilise an egg. The only one hundred per cent reliable method of contraception was abstinence.

She was pregnant.

'I'm going to be a father.' He said the words slowly, testing them out.

A father. He'd planned to start a family with Sienna, after their stint at Doctors Without Borders. Except then she'd died in the flash flood and he'd shied away from the thought of ever settling down and having a family. How could he be so selfish as to want that for himself, when Sienna would never have that chance?

'A father,' he said again, still not able to take it in.

'I'm sorry,' she whispered.

He wasn't going to let her take the blame. 'It takes two to make a baby.'

A baby.

Their baby.

'How pregnant are you?' he asked hoarsely.

'I don't know. It's early days.' Her breath hitched. 'I felt funny today. Everything smelled. My tea tasted disgusting. I thought I was premenstrual.'

'But you did a test?'

She closed her eyes. 'I thought it was negative,' she whispered. 'And then I looked again…and it was positive.'

Pregnant.

With his baby.

And Marco suddenly knew exactly what to do, because now everything was clicking into place. 'It's OK, *tesoro*. We'll get married.'

'No.'

He stared at her, shocked. 'What do you mean, no? You're expecting my baby. Unless… Were you thinking…?' He couldn't quite bring himself to say the words. She'd said a while back that she didn't want children. Was she really thinking of having a termination?

She was shaking again. 'There's a fifty per cent chance that this baby's inherited my NF2—and it's a variable condition. You can't tell how badly any individual's going to be affected. I'm reasonably OK, but supposing the baby's affected much more badly than I am? Tumours in the brain can cause fits, vision problems, difficulty with balance. Or spinal tumours on the neck might make it hard for him to blink or smile or swallow. Or he might have spinal tumours like mine, except they might develop at a much younger age—he could end up in a wheelchair. And it's all my fault.'

He could see the panic in her face. And she was thinking about the worst possible scenarios. He needed to get some balance into this, right now. 'There's also a fifty per cent chance that he or she will be absolutely fine.'

'But we don't *know*, Marco. We don't know anything. It's not like an exam, when you know whether you've worked hard enough and you've got a pretty good idea how you did. This is completely out of my—*our*—control.'

He forced himself to say the words. 'So you want a termination?'

She swallowed hard. 'I've been thinking about it all afternoon. How can I destroy a life? It's not what I want. I can't do it. And yet I'll never forgive myself if I've passed this—this *disease* on. Whatever way I look at it, I'll be doing the wrong thing. I can't kill our baby. But I can't... I can't...' The words choked off.

He wrapped his arms round her. 'I don't know what to say. Except it's my baby too, and we'll get married and deal with this together.'

'That's your sense of responsibility talking. It's not fair to you.' She dragged in another breath. 'I don't want you to do what you think is the right thing, and end up resenting me and the baby for holding you back and making you change your plans.'

'I wouldn't resent you.'

'Maybe not right now, you wouldn't. But how do you know how you'll feel in a year's time, five, ten?' She shook her head. 'We've never discussed the future. I mean, this thing between us—we never made each other any promises. We said we'd just see where it takes us.'

'We have—and it's brought us here. It's given us both something we've never expected.'

'I never even asked you if you wanted to have a fam—' Her voice broke.

He stroked her face. 'Yes, I did. Sienna and I were going to try for a family after we'd worked at Doctors Without Borders. And then...' He sighed. 'After she died, I put it out of my head. Even when I started to date again, it wasn't something I let myself think about. It seemed wrong, planning a future when she didn't have one any more.' He drew her close. 'This feels as if I've been given a second chance at happiness. A chance to have that family I always wanted.' He paused. 'Except you don't want children. You told me that weeks ago.'

Her eyes filled with tears. 'I wasn't being completely honest with you about that. I...I did want children. I wanted to feel a baby growing inside me, those little flutters when the baby first kicked, even the heartburn and the backache. I wanted it all. I told myself it was fine being just an aunt, but it wasn't true. I envied my sister and my sister-in-law like mad. Seeing a new life, knowing you've created it—it must be so amazing.'

'So what made you change your mind about wanting children?' he asked softly.

'The NF2.' She dragged in a breath. 'I asked my consultant what it meant for the future. He said if we had IVF we could screen the embryo before implantation and make sure the baby hadn't inherited my NF2. And pregnancy...it can affect my condition. You know as well as I do, pregnancy hormones can affect a lot of medical conditions, make things speed up or slow down.

In my case the tumours can grow faster or larger. They can cause extra problems with nerves. And as soon as Craig found out the risks, he was dead against the idea of having a baby.'

'What about adopting a child?'

'Or fostering. I suggested it. He refused flatly. It was as if something just shut off inside him. He said he didn't want a family. Ever. And that I was selfish to want a child.' She bit her lip. 'Except he wasn't telling me the whole truth, either. A month after he left me, I found out he'd moved in with someone else.' Her voice was so cracked, Marco could barely make out the words. 'And she was three months pregnant with his baby.'

Marco swore. 'And he made you believe that the break-up of your marriage was your fault, when all the time he'd been unfaithful to you?'

'It *was* my fault,' she said, looking desperately sad and tired. 'If I'd been normal, if I hadn't had NF2, he wouldn't have needed to look elsewhere. He wouldn't have needed to find someone who could give him a baby without complications.'

'No *way*,' Marco said firmly. 'He wasn't man enough to give you the support you needed, when you needed it. He didn't deserve a bright, warm, gorgeous woman like you—and you are gorgeous, Sydney, you really are. Inside and out.' He paused. 'I'm not so sure that I'm good enough for you, but I'll do my best to be.'

She frowned. 'Not good enough?'

He couldn't tell her now. She had enough to deal with. But he'd explain later. And in the meantime he'd try his hardest to give her the support she needed, the support she deserved. 'It takes two to make a baby. And I'm going to support you. Starting with going with you to see your consultant and seeing if things have changed since you last thought about starting a family.'

'Five years ago. Just before I started here.'

'Medicine changes, *tesoro*. Maybe there are new answers now. But if there aren't, it doesn't matter, because I'll be here.'

'But you're going back to Italy in three months' time.'

'Was,' he corrected. 'I can extend my secondment.'

'But I thought you really missed Italy.'

He shrugged. 'The situation's different now.'

'But—'

The only way he could think of to stop her talking and make her see that he really did want to be here was to kiss her. For long enough that they were both breathless.

'Things change,' he said softly, 'and you have to learn to compromise to deal with the changes. We're going to have to roll with this. Right now, we're both shocked and in a place where we don't have a clue what we do next. But sitting here in the middle of the night, getting upset and not being able to make an informed decision, isn't going to be good for either of us.' Or the baby, though he didn't quite dare add that. 'We're both on early shift tomorrow. We need to get some sleep. Come back to bed, *tesoro*. I don't have any answers right now, but maybe if we sleep on it we'll be in a better place to make decisions tomorrow.'

She nestled closer. 'I know you're right. I just wish…'

'We'll work it out,' he said. 'Together.'

Though, he didn't get much sleep that night, and he was pretty sure that Sydney was faking it, too. Her breathing wasn't quite deep and even enough to be that of genuine sleep.

Quite how they were going to work this out, he had no idea. It scared the hell out of him. Even apart from his fear of letting himself love someone and lose them again, the way he'd lost Sienna… He'd let his wife down, and now he was being given a second chance. Would he end up letting Sydney down, too? Or could he get it right, this time?

The only way to find out was to give it a try.

And he was going to give it his very, very best shot. To give Sydney the family she deserved and the love she deserved. Somehow.

CHAPTER TEN

No LEMONS. No ginger. No peppermint teabags—nothing that would settle Sydney's stomach. In the end, Marco gave up looking through the cupboards and the fridge. He put some dry crackers on a plate and filled a glass with water, then took them in to Sydney.

'How are you feeling?' he asked.

'OK.'

Considering that she was pale, with dark smudges under her eyes, he didn't believe her.

'You?' she asked.

'Fine.' It was just as big a lie, and he could see from her expression that she knew it, too. 'Eat your crackers. They'll stop you feeling sick.'

'Thank you.' But she only nibbled at them. And she crumbled one of them completely.

He sat on the edge of the bed and took her hand. 'You're brooding about something. Talk to me.'

'When I had my annual check-up, I had an MRI scan.' She bit her lip. 'And pregnant women aren't supposed to be scanned in their first trimester, because of the risks to the baby.'

'OK. Firstly, it's early days and you had no idea that you were pregnant, so don't blame yourself. Secondly, it's a theoretical risk. The chances are, everything's absolutely fine.' He squeezed her hand. 'I know you're worried, and I know why you're worried. But, until we've talked to the consultant, we're coming from a position of ignorance and we're probably scaring ourselves over nothing.'

'I know,' she said, sounding miserable. 'But I can't help it, Marco. The fear's like a fog all around me, and I can't fight my way through it.'

'Talk to your consultant today,' he said. 'Get an appointment. I'll come with you.' He kissed her lightly. 'And we'd better get moving, or we'll be late for work.'

And, because babies and children were uppermost in her mind, it seemed that it ended up being Sydney's day for treating them. A toddler with a bead stuck up her nose; another who'd cracked her head against her grandmother's piano hard enough to have a deep gash needing stitches; a young lad who'd fallen over on the playing field and stretched out an arm to save himself, ending up with a Colles' fracture.

But the one that really got to her was the five-year-old who'd gashed his arm.

'I'm going to clean it, then put some magic cream on it to numb it,' she said to him, 'and then I'll be able to stitch it up and you'll be absolutely fine.'

The little boy was convinced that it was still going to hurt, and screamed the place down. But the cut was too long for her to be able to glue it or use skin closure strips, so there was no alternative to stitches.

'Sweetheart, the doctor's not going to hurt you. She's going to make you feel better,' his dad said, cuddling the child. 'And do you know how I know? She's magic.'

The little boy continued roaring his head off.

'Watch. She's so magic that I can make a coin appear from behind her ear.' He opened both hands wide, to show his son that they were empty, then clicked his fingers behind Sydney's ear and produced a coin. 'See? She's magic. So the magic cream she put on your arm will definitely work.'

At that, the little boy became calmer. 'Are you sure, Daddy?'

'Yes, sweetheart, I'm sure. Everything's going to be just fine.' His father stroked his hair back from his tear-stained face, and the little boy gave him a wobbly smile.

'What a gorgeous smile,' Sydney said. 'Did you feel that?'

'Feel what?'

'I just put the first stitch in,' she said.

The little boy looked at his arm, to check that she was really telling him the truth. 'But it didn't hurt.'

'Your dad's right. It's magic, so it won't hurt,' she said with a smile, and finished suturing the cut. 'There we go. All done. And I think you deserve a bravery sticker.' She took a small sheet of stickers from her pocket. 'Do you want to choose one?'

'Thank you,' the little boy whispered, and chose one of a lion with a plaster on his nose.

'If there's any sign of infection, you'll need to bring him back in.' She quickly went through the signs of infection with the little boy's father. 'Other than that, come back in a week or so and we can take the stitches out. And I promise that doesn't hurt, either.' She ruffled the little boy's hair. 'Well done for being so brave.' She smiled at his father. 'And I was very impressed with the magic trick.'

'I normally use them on the kids at school. If we've had a good day, I'll do a couple of magic tricks at the end of the day,' he said.

She could imagine Marco doing something like that. Learning magic tricks to delight his child, and comforting him and distracting him the way this little boy's father had just done. It made her heart ache. Would they get the chance to be a family? Could this work out? The questions spun round and round in her head, and she was no closer to finding an answer.

She managed to get an appointment to see her consultant, later that afternoon, and Marco came with her.

'Well—congratulations,' Michael Fraser said. 'You didn't say anything the other week.'

'Because I didn't know I was. We didn't exactly plan this to happen,' Sydney said. She took a deep breath. 'I've read up on NF2 in pregnancy.'

'No doubt scaring yourself silly in the process,' Michael said wryly. 'Worst-case scenario, yes, your tumours might grow faster—particularly the ones on your vestibular nerves, so you might start getting tinnitus and some hearing loss. But you also might sail through this pregnancy with nothing more than any other pregnant women faces—morning sickness, backache and indigestion.'

Marco's fingers tightened round hers. 'How will you know if Sydney's condition changes?'

'We'll monitor her more regularly. I'll book you in for more appointments with me, Sydney,' Michael said, 'and I think, rather than using your GP and midwife for antenatal care, I'm going to refer you to Theo Petrakis in the maternity department here.'

She nodded. 'I know Theo. I've sent patients up to him before.'

'So you already know how good he is.' Michael looked pleased. 'Hopefully that will help to reassure you a bit.'

'Yes. As long as keeping an eye on me doesn't mean sending me for more MRI scans.' Sydney swallowed hard. 'The one I had the other week—'

'Is highly unlikely to be a problem for the baby, if that's what you've been reading up about. So try to put it out of your mind and stop worrying about it,' Michael cut in gently.

'What worries me the most,' Sydney said quietly, 'is whether the baby has NF2. There's a fifty per cent risk of inheriting it.'

'We can test for that, when you're fifteen weeks—I assume you know what an amniocentesis involves?'

'Technically.' She shrugged. 'Obviously I haven't been through it myself or done the procedure on anyone else.'

'Because you work in a different speciality,' Michael said. 'If the chromosome is affected, we can't tell you how severe the condition will be—but at least you'll be able to prepare yourselves. Remember, though, a fifty per cent chance of inheriting it also means a fifty per cent chance of *not* inheriting it.'

Again, Marco squeezed her hand, as if to say, *See? It's going to be fine.*

'I'll see you in a month, and in the meantime I'll book you in with Theo. You know where I am if you have any questions—if you're worried about anything at all, just come and see me. Either or both of you.'

'Thank you.' Sydney blew out a breath when they left Michael's office. 'I'm scared, Marco.'

'I know, *tesoro*.' He kept his fingers firmly laced through hers.

'Supposing the baby's affected?'

'You're building bridges to trouble. You said earlier, it's not like an exam, when you have a rough idea how well you've done. This is something we can't change. Try to focus on the fifty per cent chance of the baby not having NF2.'

'I'll try.' Though it was easier said than done. It was easier at work, when she had to focus on her patients and had no time to think about anything else, but when she was off duty it loomed uppermost in her mind.

Marco did his best to distract her. He continued to work through his list, taking her to the Aquarium and London Zoo and the Planetarium. And all around them, Sydney saw families. Babies and toddlers enchanted by the brightly coloured fish. Preschoolers laughing in delight as they walked through the butterfly house. Older children trying the hands-on exhibits and marvelling over the 4.5-billion-year-old meteorite.

Families.

Something she wanted so badly.

Was it so much to ask? 'No, it's not too much to ask,' he said.

She blinked. 'Did I just say that out loud?'

'No, but it was written all over your face. Longing.' He twined his fingers through hers. 'It's not too much to ask. And we're lucky, Sydney. We've been given something very, very special—the chance to be a family together.' He gestured to the people around them. 'I see them and I think, this is what it's going to be like for us.'

'What if...?' She couldn't quite bear to speak it out loud. In case she tempted Fate.

'Then we'll deal with it. I'm not saying it's going to be easy—whether our baby has NF2 or not, it's not going to be plain sailing all the time. We'll have our problems, just like all parents do. But we'll deal with it.' He smiled at her. 'Because we'll be together. And we can lean on each other.' His eyes glittered. 'Just so you know, I'm terrified that I'm not going to be a good enough father. So you're going to have days when you're going to have to reassure me, just as I'll have days when I'll need to reassure you that it's OK not to be perfect, either.' He shrugged. 'I guess we just have to take things as they come. And that's worked for us so far, hasn't it?'

'Yes,' she admitted. He hadn't said he loved her, just as she hadn't said that she loved him. But she looked forward to being with him, and she was pretty sure it was the same for him, too. So maybe he was right, and they just had to relax and take things as they came, and just trust each other to be there.

Sydney's first appointment with Theo Petrakis was hugely reassuring.

'I've looked after several mums who've had NF2. I won't lie to you and say it's going to be completely problem-free—you're a doctor and you know what your condition means. You're a high-risk mum, so you're going to be seeing me once a week, and we're going to keep a close eye on your blood pressure. But there's a pretty good chance you're going to have a healthy baby and a reasonably good pregnancy.' Theo smiled at her. 'I can put you in touch with some of my mums, if you like. Having a support group of people who understand because they've been there can really help.'

'Thank you. I'd like that,' she said.

'So. First things first. I've asked Ultrasound to fit you in for a dating scan.' He looked at Marco. 'I hope you've got tissues with you. If you haven't, I'd advise you to go and buy some.'

Marco frowned, mystified. 'Why?'

'Put it this way, even though I've seen hundreds of scans before, the first time I saw my own baby on the screen, I had to blink back the tears. It's incredibly moving. Like nothing you can imagine.'

Half an hour and three glasses of water later, Marco and Sydney were called in to the ultrasound suite. Sydney held his hand tightly as the ultrasonographer squeezed radio-conductive gel over her abdomen and ran the transceiver head over it.

'We have a good picture,' she said.

Marco stared at the screen, watching the tiny foetus whizzing around inside Sydney's womb, its tiny heart beating so strongly...

And the last of the barriers he'd put up round his heart simply collapsed. Theo had warned him that this was moving—but he hadn't said the half of it. It blew Marco away. This was his child. His baby. His and Sydney's. A tiny life that they'd made together, curled up inside her. A little miracle they hadn't asked for but they'd been given.

Protectiveness surged through him, shocking him

with its intensity. He'd never, ever felt before that he
would willingly lay his life down for someone else—but
he'd do it for this baby. And it was terrifying.

'Marco, you're hurting my hand,' Sydney said softly.

'Sorry.' He released his grip. 'That's…that's…' He
was lost for words. How could he explain how amazing
this was, to see their unborn child? It was as if he'd just
been dropped into a slot—and it fitted. Felt *right*.

'You're seven weeks,' the ultrasonographer said as
she finished taking measurements. 'So you'll be having
a Valentine's baby.'

Marco couldn't think of anything he wanted more.

Though he could see the conflict in Sydney's face.
The longing. Clearly she wanted this baby as much as
he did, felt that same surge of protective love for their
child. But he also knew that she wouldn't be able to
relax completely, wouldn't be able to let herself give
their child all that deep, deep love she felt, until she
was absolutely sure that the baby hadn't inherited her
condition. Not because she was prejudiced against disability—he'd seen the care she'd taken with disabled
patients in their department—but because she wouldn't
ever be able to forgive herself for passing on that disability. She'd always blame herself.

How could he make her see that it didn't matter?
That they'd both love their child, no matter what, and
they'd be able to face the problems and cope with things
together?

Maybe it was time he told her the truth about
Sienna. Faced up to things himself: he, too, had spent
years not being able to forgive himself. It was a risk:
once she knew the truth about him, she might not

want him there any more. But he was going to fight for her. Because she was worth it.

At the end of their shift, Marco looked serious.

'Is everything OK?' Sydney asked.

'I need to talk to you about something.'

A flicker of fear ran through her. Was this where it all went wrong and history repeated itself? Had Marco had time to think about it and decided that the complications would be too much for him?

'Sure,' she said, trying to sound neutral.

'Let's go to the park. Find a quiet spot.'

The worry and anticipation grew as she walked with him through the park, found a quiet spot by the lake.

'You were honest with me,' he said, 'about what happened with Craig. And I need to—to be honest with you about Sienna.'

'You don't have to tell me anything.'

'I want to,' he said simply. 'Because I don't want any more barriers between us. And I'll warn you now, it's not good.' He dragged in a breath. 'And afterwards, when you know...I'll understand if you change your mind about me.'

She frowned. 'Why would I do that?'

'Because it's my fault that Sienna died.'

No way. She didn't believe that for a second. But he clearly needed to tell her the truth, and the least she could do was be there for him and not judge, the same way that he'd been there for her when she'd told him about Craig. She reached over to take his hand. 'I'm listening,' she said softly.

'I met her when I was a student. It's a cliché, but I fell in love with her the first day we met. Well, what an eighteen-year-old thinks of as love. We studied together, we worked together—and we knew we wanted to be together. We got married the week after we graduated.'

What an eighteen-year-old thinks of as love. Sydney knew how that felt. OK, so she'd met Craig when she was twenty, but it had been the same thing for her. That rush of passion, the joy, the hope. And they hadn't even waited until she'd graduated before they'd got married. They'd thought they'd be together for ever. *For richer, for poorer, in sickness and in health...* What a joke that had turned out to be.

But it had obviously been different for Marco. It really had been, *until death us do part.*

'I worked in the emergency department, and Sienna was a paediatrician. We both thought we'd got all the time in the world to start a family, so we concentrated on our careers. Then she saw this documentary, and she couldn't get the pictures out of her head. She told me she wanted to do a stint at Doctors Without Borders, so she could help people and make a real difference. And I knew what she meant—I liked the idea, too. It was why I became a doctor, to make things right. We planned to do a year with Doctors Without Borders, then come back to Italy and start a family.'

No wonder he'd gone all distant on her when she'd asked him if he'd thought about working for Doctors Without Borders. She squeezed his hand.

'But then I was offered a promotion. It meant I'd be working with one of the best emergency specialists in Italy. I'd learn such a lot—I'd be able to give so much more to my patients. So if I delayed that year out at Doctors Without Borders, just for six months... Could I be that selfish and put my career first, knowing how much she was looking forward to working with me for Doctors Without Borders?'

Sydney knew what she would've done in those circumstances. Told him to stay and that they'd do their Doctors Without Borders stint later. 'What did Sienna think about it?'

'She saw how much I wanted to do it. So we compromised. I'd take the post, stay in Rome for six months, and then I'd follow her.' He closed his eyes. 'Three months into her service, there was a flash flood, and she was killed.'

He'd said she'd died in an accident. Sydney hadn't pushed for the details—but now she knew how tragic it had been. Sienna had died while trying to help people. Sydney stroked the pad of her thumb over the back of his hand. 'I'm so sorry.'

'The worst thing is, if I'd been out there with her, the way I was supposed to be—instead of being selfish and following my own needs—it wouldn't have happened.'

'How do you work that one out? Marco, nobody can stop a flash flood.'

'But I would've been able to keep her safe,' he insisted, 'so she wasn't risking her life.'

'Has it occurred to you,' she asked softly, 'that if you'd been there you might've died as well?'

He shook his head. 'I let her down.'

'No. She talked it over with you and you found a workable compromise—which is exactly what I would've done, too. OK, I didn't know her, so I can't say how she would've felt, but I *can* tell you how I would've felt in her shoes. I know what a good doctor you are, Marco, and the promotion would make you even better because you'd learn so much from the specialist. So I wouldn't have resented you for not going straight out to Doctors Without Borders with me; I would've been proud of you for making the right decision for your patients and your career.' She met his gaze. 'You know when I told you about me, and you said that nothing had changed? Well, the same goes this time round. You're a good man, Marco Ranieri. And I...' There was a huge lump in her throat. Did she tell him she loved him? But right now she didn't think he'd hear what she was saying. It'd be just words. 'I couldn't ask for a better father for my baby.'

He looked bleak. 'How can you say that? I put my own needs first. I was selfish.'

'You weren't selfish. You didn't tell her not to go. You didn't stand in her way. And if she hadn't died, you would've gone out there exactly as you agreed to do— you wouldn't have made excuses.' She sighed. 'Marco, you're expecting the impossible from yourself. Even if you'd been there, you couldn't have saved her. Yes, it was tragic that she died so young—but sometimes things just happen in life that we can't fix and wouldn't stand a chance of fixing.'

'I've tried to tell myself that,' he said.

But clearly, Sydney thought, he hadn't been able to believe it.

'I went through all the stages of grief. Denial that she was dead, anger that she'd been taken, bargaining that if I could have her back, I'd give so much to the world.' He blew out a breath. 'And then depression. Missing her so much that it was a physical pain. For six months, it was like living in the shadows. I moved house, but it didn't help—I saw her everywhere I went. Like a ghost. She haunted me. In the end, my sister dragged me out to lunch and told me that if I wanted to follow Sienna to the grave, I was going the right way about it. That, yes, it was terrible she'd died so young, but she knew Sienna and knew she wouldn't want me to waste my life the way I was doing, that she wouldn't want me to destroy myself.'

'I didn't know Sienna, so I can't speak for her,' Sydney said, 'but I'm with your sister on that. If Craig and I...if he'd been the man I thought I fell in love with, and I'd died when they operated on my spine, I wouldn't have wanted him to spend the rest of his life alone and mourning me. I would've wanted him to find someone else who loved him as much as I did. I would've wanted him to be happy.' She paused. 'Supposing it was the other way round for you—would you have wanted Sienna to spend the rest of her life alone, mourning you, no joy in her life?'

'No. I'd want her to...' his breath hitched '...to have a family who loved her.'

'There you go, then.' She stroked his face. 'That's the last stage of grief. The one you didn't talk about. Acceptance. Knowing that you can't bring her back, and nothing you could've done would've saved her. That it wasn't your fault. And that it's time to move on.'

He sighed. 'I did what Vittoria suggested. I went out. I dated. But I never let anyone close. And I couldn't get rid of the guilt—I felt so responsible. I still do. If I'd gone out there with her, or if I'd persuaded her to wait until I could go with her... So many times, I begged for time to turn back just a few short months, to give me a second chance to make things right. I used to dream of it—and then I'd wake alone.' His expression was bleak. 'It was like losing her all over again.'

'So you weren't really ready to date again,' she said softly.

'Not then, no. I felt I let Sienna down, and I lost my faith in myself.' He looked at her. 'And then came to London and I met you, and the world suddenly seemed like a different place. There weren't any memories to haunt me in London. I could enjoy just being with you. Having fun.' He paused. 'Though, if I'm honest with you, I feel a bit guilty about that. I can't even see Sienna's face any more. I can't remember what her perfume smells like. I can't remember her voice. And she was my *wife*.' He looked anguished. 'I loved her for more than a third of my life. How can I forget her just like that?'

'Because you haven't seen her for more than two years. And memories fade, on the surface. But she's still here.' Sydney put her hand over his heart. 'Exactly where she should be. Exactly where she'll always be—because part of you will always love her.'

He frowned. 'And that doesn't bother you?'

She shook her head. 'She was part of your life before you met me. I don't expect you to scrub out every memory of her and get rid of every photograph, because that's totally wrong. She helped to make you who you are now. A man who's kind and caring. A man who notices problems and fixes them quietly, without expecting lots of fuss and praise for his efforts.'

He looked at her, as if unable to believe she really thought that of him.

'It's true. And the way you make me feel—you make me feel different, too. That evening we went to the London Eye, I felt like a princess.'

'That's how I want you to feel, always.' He bit his

lip. 'I know I'm asking you to trust me, and trust's hard for you after what Craig did to you. You've been let down badly before. And I've let my partner down badly before, so I'm hardly the best person to trust. It scares the hell out of me that I'm going to let you down when you need me most.'

'You're not going to let me down.' She felt the tears fill her eyes. 'Marco, you've been there for me and supported me every minute since I told you about the baby. You've come to all my appointments with me, you've held me when I can't sleep. I couldn't ask for anything more.' She took a deep breath. 'Remember what you told me about just taking things as they come? I think you're right. Maybe that's what we need to do right now.'

'None of it matters, as long as we're together.' He wrapped his arms round her. 'I'll try my hardest not to let you down.'

'I know. And that's all I want,' she said softly.

CHAPTER ELEVEN

BUT Sydney was still waking up in the middle of the night. Every time Marco woke to find the bed empty, he knew where she'd be. In the kitchen, sipping a glass of water and trying not to bawl her eyes out. And every time, he just scooped her up, sat down and settled her on his lap, holding her close and willing her to take strength from him.

'I'm sorry. I'm trying not to brood.' She gulped. 'I just wish…'

He knew what she wished. That this baby had been planned, the embryo had been screened and she could relax and enjoy her pregnancy, without worrying that she'd passed on her condition. Even though it wasn't her fault that the gene had mutated, and it took two to make a baby, planned or accidental.

'IVF isn't an easy option, you know,' he said softly. 'And sometimes it takes several cycles until it works. One of my sister's friends went through it, and she ended up having seven cycles of treatment over three years. Vittoria says it nearly destroyed her.'

'And this is destroying me,' Sydney whispered. 'Waiting and wondering, and praying that I haven't passed on my bad chromosomes. That I haven't taken away our baby's quality of life.'

'You haven't taken away our baby's quality of life,' he reassured her. 'If he or she has NF2, for all we know, it might even be milder than you have it.'

'It's three weeks until the amnio,' she said. 'And then a two-week wait until we get the results.' She looked bleak. 'It feels like a lifetime. I just want to know. To be *sure.*' She bit her lip. 'I want this baby. I do. I don't even have the words to describe how I feel—how much I love this baby. But at the same time I'm so scared, Marco. So scared that everything's going to go wrong. That the complications are all going to be too much. I just wish…'

'I know, *tesoro.*' It wasn't easy for him, either, seeing her eaten up with fear like this. This was a time when they should be enjoying the new life they'd made, making plans, choosing nursery furniture and looking at first toys and books and tiny outfits.

He needed to distract her.

And he could only think of one thing that might work.

He had a quiet and very confidential discussion with Ellen, the next day. To his relief, she agreed with him.

'Aren't you getting up for work?' Sydney asked on the Friday morning.

'Change of duty,' he said with a shrug.

As he'd hoped, she assumed that he was on a late. The second she'd left for work, he leaped out of bed, showered and dressed, then packed for both of them. Luckily she was very organised and had a file where she kept important paperwork, so he was able to locate her passport quickly. He booked the taxi, then had just enough time to make one essential purchase before taking the taxi to the hospital with their suitcases at lunchtime.

Sydney had just seen her last patient before her break when Marco walked into the department to find her.

'Ready for lunch?' he asked.

She looked surprised. 'You came in early just to have lunch with me?'

'Something like that,' he said with a smile. Only better.

'Aren't we going to the canteen?'

'Nope.'

She frowned when she saw the taxi. 'Marco? What's going on?'

'I'm kidnapping you.'

'But you're on a late, and I still have half a shift to do.'

'I'm on a day off, and you're on leave as of...' he glanced at his watch '...about five seconds ago. I'm taking you away for a few days,' he said. 'Completely away from here. You need a break, and I know the best place in the world to relax.'

'But—I'm on duty.'

'No, you're not. Ellen's changed your duty. You're not due back until Thursday next week.'

She blinked. '*Ellen* changed my duty?'

'She's worried about you, *tesoro*,' he said softly. 'I knew you'd told her about the baby, so I had a quiet word with her the other day. And she agrees with me—a break will do you good, help to take your mind off the situation.' He smiled at her. 'And we have a taxi waiting to take us to the airport.'

'Where are we going?'

He refused to be drawn. 'I'll tell you when we're about to board.'

'Marco, I...'

'Just enjoy this, *tesoro*,' he said softly. 'You have a lot you're worrying about and you need distracting. And this is the best way I can think of doing that.'

'But—I haven't packed.'

'I packed for both of us. If I missed anything, then I'll get it for you at our destination,' he told her.

'I don't know what to say.'

He kissed her lightly. 'You just say "Yes", and get in the taxi.'

It wasn't until they got to check-in that Sydney finally found out where they were going. 'Naples.'

'That's the nearest airport to Capri.' He was taking her home. To *his* home.

'I've booked us into a hotel in Sorrento.' He squeezed her hand. 'I thought staying with my parents might be a bit too much pressure for you. Though we do need to call in and see my family while we're in Italy,' he added, 'or they'll never forgive me.'

He'd thought of everything. 'Marco, I...' She felt the tears well up.

'Don't cry, *tesoro*. Everything's going to be fine.'

Their flight was on time, and he'd arranged a hire car at the airport. 'My sister's using my car while I'm in England, and it's not fair of me to demand it back at zero notice,' he said. 'I suppose we could've taken the train, but I love the drive round the coast.'

She smiled. 'And trust you to make it an open-topped car.'

'Well, it'd be a pity to waste the sunshine,' he said

with a grin. He drove them out of the city. 'Look to your left.'

A huge mountain loomed over them—and then she realised what it was. 'Vesuvius?'

'Yes, and you can see her from the whole peninsula. She'll follow us all the way to Sorrento. We can walk up the volcano later in the week, if you like; there are stunning views from the top.'

Sydney enjoyed the drive, despite the road being so twisting and narrow. The view was spectacular, with houses scattered on the cliffside leading down to a perfect turquoise sea. When they arrived at the hotel, she found that he'd booked what she suspected was the honeymoon suite; it was right at the top of the hotel, secluded, with its own balcony and stunning views over the sea.

'Is that Capri?' she asked, gesturing to the island in the distance.

'Ischia. Capri's a little further round to the left.'

When she unpacked, she discovered that he'd packed everything she would've put in the case herself. There was enough time to shower and change before dinner on a terrace overlooking the sunset; and the food was fantastic.

'Marco, thank you for this. Though I ought to p—'

'No,' he cut in, second-guessing her, 'this is my treat. You're not paying for *anything*. We're having a few days away where we don't have to think and we don't have to worry—just the two of us, no pressure, so we can relax and enjoy it. It's the complete opposite of London, here—slow and easy, not rush, rush, rush.'

When they made love that night, his touch was very tender, very sweet. He undressed her slowly, stroking her skin as he uncovered it and following the path of his hands with his mouth. He cupped her breasts and teased her hardening nipples with the pads of his thumbs until her breathing grew uneven, then dipped his head and took one nipple into his mouth, teasing it with his tongue and his teeth until she slid her hands into his hair, urging him on.

'Marco, I need you now,' she whispered.

He gently laid her on the bed against the pillows, stripped off his clothes in a matter of seconds and let them lay where they fell. 'Now?' he asked.

In answer, she drew his head down to hers and kissed him, hard.

Slowly, slowly, he entered her, keeping eye contact all the way; the sheer desire in his expression made her melt. She wrapped her legs round his waist, pulling him deeper. All she could think of was him, the way he made her feel. His kisses were sweet yet intense at the same time, giving and demanding in equal measure.

As her climax hit, she cried out his name; she heard his answering cry, muffled against her shoulder.

He was holding her so tightly, as if he'd never let her go. It had never been quite like this before; was it because they were here, in Italy, or was it because things were changing between them again? Had he finally come to terms with his own nightmares? She didn't want to spoil the moment by asking him. But as she relaxed in his arms she held on to the thought that maybe, just maybe, he was falling in love with her, the way she was falling for him.

They were on the top floor and nobody could see into their room; he'd left the curtains open, and she could see the stars against the inky sky. *Star light, star bright, first star I see tonight...* The old rhyme echoed in her head. And she knew exactly what she'd wish for. To be a real family, with Marco and their baby—without the spectre of NF2.

For the first time in weeks, Sydney actually slept properly, and the next morning at breakfast she felt more human than she had for ages. The nausea had gone; traditionally, this was the time when women bloomed. And here, away from their usual routine, and with Marco being so tender, she felt as if she was really blooming.

'No coffee for me, thanks,' she said to the waiter. 'Just orange juice will be lovely.' Especially as it was freshly squeezed.

'Do you mind if I have coffee, or is the smell too much for you?' Marco asked.

'It's fine.'

'Grazie, tesoro.'

While Sydney stuck to toast, plain yoghurt and a juicy-looking nectarine, Marco indulged in the pastries. 'This is one thing you definitely can't find in England.'

'What, cake for breakfast?' she teased.

'Pasticiotti, if you please—I can never decide between the lemon ricotta and the vanilla filling.'

She eyed his plate. 'So you have both.'

He grinned. 'It's a proper Italian breakfast. I'll work it off in the pool, this afternoon. I thought I'd take you to Vesuvius this morning, if you'd like a walk. It's not too strenuous, and if we go now we can avoid the hottest part of the day.'

'That'd be lovely.'

He drove them back towards Naples, then turned off up a very narrow and twisting road; there was barely enough room for the cars and buses to pass each other, and there were several places where Marco had to reverse to let a bus through.

'I'm glad you're the one driving, not me,' she said feelingly.

At last they reached the car park. 'The air gets a bit thin, so just say if you need to stop. We'll take it steady,' Marco said.

The path looked as if it went in wide zigzags and didn't slope too sharply; but clearly appearances were deceptive because there were two people handing out stout sticks at the bottom of the path.

'I thought you said it wasn't strenuous?' she asked.

'It isn't that bad, but can be a bit slippery underfoot, with all the little bits of lava on the path. The sticks help you keep your balance.'

They sat down on one of the benches halfway up the path to look out over the Bay of Naples and the stunning view. The slopes of the volcano were covered in trees and bushes with yellow flowers.

Strange to think this was a live volcano they were walking up; right now it seemed just like any other mountain. But when they got to the top, she could smell the sulphur and see the yellow deposits on the far side of the crater. Then she looked down into the crater and saw little puffs of smoke. 'Wow—that's actually steam coming from the vents!' It was as if she understood the real power of nature for the first time; that crater had been filled with hundreds and hundreds of tons of rock, and it had all been blasted out by the force of the eruption. 'This is awesome,' she said, 'in the true sense of the word.'

He smiled. 'It's been a while since I came here, but I know what you mean. My parents brought us here when we were small, and I can still remember the first time. It just blew me away.' He laughed. 'Pun not quite intended. And, of course, I had to have an ornament made out of lava. I still have the little salamander somewhere.' He bought one for her at the souvenir stall at the top of the slope. 'He'll remind you of Vesuvius.'

They were on their way back down the slope when they saw a small child who'd clearly fallen over and grazed her knees. Her father was looking anxious and her mother was frantically looking through her bag—for plasters, Sydney guessed, and the worried look on the woman's face told her that the hunt was unsuccessful.

She tugged at Marco's hand. 'I have plasters and wipes—but if they don't speak English I'll need you to translate for me.'

'Of course, *tesoro.*'

They went over to the parents; Marco established that they were Italian, and explained that he and Sydney were both doctors. While she took the wipes and plasters from her bag, Marco soothed the child and sang an Italian song—a tune she recognised, but she had no idea what the words were. The child clearly knew it as she joined in, her high voice harmonising with Marco's rich tenor.

Gently, she cleaned up the little girl's knees. This was what it would be like to be a family with Marco. She could imagine him singing with their child, the way he was with this little girl. He'd make such a great dad. They'd make a great family, because this baby really would be loved. So much. By both of them.

'*Mille grazie,*' the little girl's mother said.

'*Prego,*' Marco answered with a smile.

Despite the stout stick, Sydney nearly slipped on the

way down; Marco caught her arm to stop her falling. 'OK?' he asked.

She smiled at him. 'I'm fine. Thanks for rescuing me.'

'No problem.' He smiled back. 'When you were patching up that little girl's knees, you went all dreamy for a moment. What were you thinking?'

'That you're going to make such a great dad. You'll sing our baby's tears away.'

He laughed. 'I'll certainly give it a go. And you're going to make a great mum. Practical and kind and warm and...our baby's going to love you so much.'

Maybe, she thought. If she could only keep her fears at bay.

'It's going to work out, *tesoro*,' he said softly. 'Whatever happens, we'll cope—because we're together. Trust me.'

Looking into his dark, dark eyes, Sydney believed that she could trust him. That maybe, just maybe, he was right.

Once they were safely down at the bottom and had handed in their sticks, Marco drove them back to the hotel. 'It's the hottest part of the day. Definitely time for a siesta.'

She was grateful for the break, especially as the room was air-conditioned; and the nap really revived her. In the evening, Marco took her to a restaurant with a fabulous terrace overlooking the sea—and inevitably in the shadow of Vesuvius. The food was fabulous, and she was delighted to discover that the ice-cream sundae she'd ordered came shaped like the volcano, with sparklers on the top. 'How lovely!'

'So is the distraction working?' Marco asked.

She took his hand across the table. 'Thank you, it's helping a lot—and you're right, this is a beautiful part of the world.'

'It's the most romantic place in Italy,' he said. 'Though I admit to being a tiny bit biased.'

'I love it here,' she said. 'I can see why it means so much to you.' And to think that he was choosing to stay in London, with her, rather than coming home to Italy... it was humbling, and at the same time it made her feel warm inside. Cherished. *Loved*. He hadn't actually said the words, but he didn't need to. It was in the way he acted towards her. The way he made time for her. The way he encouraged her to focus away from her fears and towards the deep, deep love she felt for their baby.

On Sunday morning, they had another lazy breakfast. 'Should we visit your parents today?' she asked.

He shook his head. 'No way are we going to Capri on a Sunday in the middle of summer. I'd rather wait until tomorrow; it'll be less crowded and a much more comfortable journey.'

They spent the day pottering about; Sydney sat on one of the recliner chairs under the orange trees and watched Marco swimming in the hotel's pool. She wasn't surprised that he was attracting admiring glances from the other women around the pool; he really was gorgeous, and his smile was enough to make any woman's knees go weak.

She found herself wondering, would she have a little boy who looked like him? Or a girl with his beautiful dark eyes? Then she realised that she automatically cupped one hand over her abdomen—just like any other pregnant woman, wanting to protect her unborn child. Cherishing it. Bonding with the little life growing inside her.

Later that day, they wandered through the old town, hand in hand; they could hear someone singing.

'My dad used to sing that when I was small. *Torna a Surriento.*' He began singing along with it, his beautiful tenor in counterpoint to the baritone.

'That's lovely,' she said when he'd finished.

'It always makes me think of here,' he said.

She found herself relaxing and almost, *almost* able to forget her worries—sitting in a café with Marco, drinking freshly squeezed orange juice, and trying the *sfogliatelle*, crispy pastries filled with a mixture of ricotta cheese and lemon. And a walk along the marina before dinner, as the sun began to set, was just perfect.

On Monday, they caught the hydrofoil over to Capri, and took the funicular railway through the lemon groves up to the main part of the town. Marco bought flowers and chocolates in the main square, then found a taxi to take them to his parents' house. She was amused to see that the taxi was open-topped, albeit with a striped awning to protect the passengers from the sun.

'Marco, I don't speak any Italian,' she reminded him when the taxi pulled up outside the address Marco had given to the driver.

'That's not a problem. Everyone in my family speaks good English. And we're not staying all day, *tesoro*—just for a little while, to say hello.'

As the taxi pulled up, nerves swamped her. 'Marco, have you told them that you and I are…?' She hadn't told her family about the baby, yet. Or her closest friends.

'No, I haven't. They know we're friends. Colleagues.

That you need a break. That's all they need to know. They won't pressure you,' he said. 'I promise.'

He paid the taxi driver, then ushered her into the house. A spaniel came bouncing up to them, barking, and Marco crouched down briefly to make a fuss of him. '*Tesoro*, this is Ciccio—who's an old softie and just makes a lot of noise to pretend he's a tough dog.'

The spaniel rolled over to have his tummy rubbed, his ears flopping over his face, and Sydney couldn't help smiling.

'Marco, *amore*!' An elegantly dressed woman who was clearly Marco's mother came into the hallway and hugged him warmly.

Marco introduced them swiftly. 'Mamma, this is Sydney. Sydney, this is my mother, Zita.'

Zita hugged Sydney, too. 'Very nice to meet you.'

'You, too,' Sydney said shyly.

'Is this your first time in Capri?'

'Yes.'

'Then you must make Marco take you to Monte Solaro. The views are amazing. Come and sit in the garden with us. Can I get you a cold drink? Juice, sparkling water?'

'Juice would be lovely, thank you.'

'I'll get it, Mamma,' Marco said. 'Sydney, go and sit down.'

Zita introduced Sydney to Salvatore, Marco's father—who was very much an older version of Marco—and then Marco appeared with a tray containing glasses and a jug of juice.

The garden overlooked the sea, with the inevitable view of Vesuvius; bougainvillea grew everywhere, as

well as beautiful blue trumpet-like flowers that Zita
told her were morning glory.

Talking to Marco's parents was as easy as talking to
her own, Sydney discovered; they had the same warmth
and kindness she liked so much in Marco.

Ciccio barked again and dashed off into the house; a
couple of moments later, two more people joined them.

'Sydney, this is Vittoria, my sister; and Roberto,
my brother,' Marco said, greeting them both warmly.
'Vittoria, Roberto, this is Sydney.'

They, too, spoke English and included Sydney in
the conversation as if they'd known her for years, instead of only just having met her. Exactly as her own
family would be with Marco, and Sydney felt a throb
of guilt at keeping him such a secret. Especially given
her pregnancy.

Zita insisted that they all stay for lunch, which they
ate in the garden. 'Proper Caprese food,' she said.
'Ravioli filled with *caiotta*, parmesan and marjoram;
chiummenzana...' she gestured to the bowl of tomato
sauce '...salad, bread. Help yourselves.'

'This is fabulous,' Sydney said after the first
mouthful.

Zita looked pleased. 'I grow my own herbs, and
Salvatore grows the tomatoes.'

They finished with *torta caprese*. 'It's traditional—
almond and chocolate cake,' Marco told her.

'And it's fantastic. Thank you so much,' Sydney said.

'Prego,' Zita said with a smile.

Although she hadn't allowed anyone to help her prepare lunch, Zita did allow Vittoria and Sydney to do the
washing up afterwards.

'It's the first time I've seen Marco happy since—'
Vittoria stopped abruptly, looking worried.

'Since Sienna?' Sydney asked lightly.

Vittoria's eyes were wary. 'He told you about her?'

'Yes. And it's so tragic that he lost her like that.'

'She was lovely. Very warm and sweet, kind.' Vittoria
smiled wryly. 'Which isn't very tactful of me, singing
her praises to you.'

'That's not a problem,' Sydney said. 'Actually, that's
what I thought she was like. I wouldn't expect him to
choose someone cold or selfish.'

'No.' Vittoria regarded her. 'I know it's the first time
we've met, but you have a lot in common with her. The
same warmth, the same kindness. And I'm glad my
brother's found someone who'll love him the way he
deserves.'

Sydney felt her eyes widen. 'He told you?'

'He didn't need to. I could tell by the way you look at
each other.' Vittoria held up one hand. 'I promise, none
of us will say anything until he's ready to tell us officially. We'll be tactful. But I'm glad. I've been so worried about him, especially since he left for England. His
emails are always cheerful, and so are his phone calls,
but unless you can see someone's eyes...' She shook
her head. 'I worried that he was really unhappy, but he
was putting on a brave face because he was trying to
stop us worrying.'

Sydney couldn't help smiling. 'You always do worry
about your family. I'm the same with my brother and
sister—even though I'm the baby out of the three of us.'

'I hope we're going to be friends,' Vittoria said.

'So do I.'

'Good.' Vittoria hugged her warmly. 'And he's a good man. He'll make you happy.'

He already does, Sydney thought. *He already does.*

'Mamma's right, I should show you Monte Solaro before we go back on the hydrofoil,' Marco said when they took their leave—and when Zita had pressed several wrapped slices of the *torte caprese* on them.

They took another taxi to Anacapri and then joined the queue for the chairlift.

As Sydney watched the people at the front of the queue, she realised that the bar across the chair wasn't locked in. 'Are you sure it's safe?'

He looked at her. 'Ah. I forgot you were scared of heights.'

'I'm not scared of heights. It was just walking backwards into nothing that spooked me. But in England that bar would be locked in. Safely.'

'It's fine, *tesoro*. Just hold on to the side of the chair if you're worried. Do you want me to go first?' he asked.

'I...' She thought about brazening it out, and gave him a wry smile. 'Yes, please. So you're there to meet me at the other end.'

He smiled. 'The views are worth it, *tesoro*, I promise.'

The slope seemed gentle at first, then suddenly became very steep—but as the ride progressed, she found herself relaxing more. By the time she arrived at the top, she was no longer gripping the side of the chair with white knuckles.

Marco was waiting for her; he took her hand and walked with her over to the railings.

'Wow. You're right, this is stunning.' There was a

sheer drop below them. 'It feels like looking over the edge of the world. And the colour of the sea... It's beautiful, Marco.'

Marco's hand closed round the box in his pocket. 'The edge of the world,' he said. 'The perfect place. Sydney...' He took a deep breath. 'I like you.'

'I like you, too.'

He shook his head. 'That's not what I meant to say. So stupid. I had all the words in my head. I rehearsed them for ages—and they're just *gone*.'

'What words?' She looked mystified.

'I...I like you. I like the way you're gentle with patients and you're patient with me. I like the way you think on your feet. I like the way you see the good in people.' She'd seen the good in him when he hadn't been able to see it himself. He kept his gaze fixed on hers. 'I like waking up with you, your smile being the first thing I see in the morning. I like going to sleep with you, the warmth of your skin being the last thing I'm aware of at night. And you make me want to be a better man.'

'Oh, Marco.' Her eyes glittered with tears. 'You don't need to be a better man. You're fine just as you are. You remember that song you sang me, that night?'

He remembered. About her being amazing, just the way she was.

'That goes for you, too,' she said softly.

It gave him enough hope to continue. 'I know this might seem fast, but I've known for a while how I feel about you.' He took a deep breath. 'I want to be with you, Sydney. I want to make a family with you, be with you for the rest of our days.' He dropped down on one knee and took the box from his pocket. 'I love you, and I want to make a life with you—and, God willing, our baby. Will you marry me?' He flipped the lid on the box.

She looked at the ring—a princess-cut tanzanite in a simple platinum setting—and a tear slid down her cheek.

'Sydney?' *Please don't let me have misjudged this. Please don't let her say no*, he begged silently.

'You love me?'

He nodded. 'I knew, that night on the London Eye. I guess I was still a bit in denial—I was still a bit of a mess—but I knew you were special. That you really meant something to me. I'm not going to forget Sienna or dismiss what we had, but you've helped me lay all the ghosts to rest. I'm ready to move on, and you've shown me that it's possible to be happy again. That happiness is there, and all you have to do is reach out and grab it with both hands. We can do that. Together.'

'You really want to marry me,' she whispered.

'Because I love you. Not because of a sense of responsibility. I love you, I love our unborn child, and whatever we face in the future I know we'll cope with it because we belong together.'

'After Craig, I never thought I'd risk my heart again,' she said. 'I never wanted to put myself in a place where I'd be vulnerable, where someone could hurt me. But you...you're different. I can trust you. You've been there for me every time I've needed you.' She took a deep breath. 'I love you, too. And I want to be a family with you.'

'So that's a yes?'

'That's a definite yes.'

He took her hand, kissed her ring finger, then slid the ring onto her finger. Then he stood up, picked her up and whirled her round. 'You've just made me the happiest man in the world.' He paused. 'My family liked you, by the way. A lot.'

'I liked them, too.' She smiled ruefully. 'I really should introduce you to my family. I guess I just didn't want to say anything until...'

She didn't have to finish. He knew what she meant. Until they knew the amnio results.

'We can keep it quiet for a while longer, if that's what you want. I won't take it personally,' he said. 'I know how you feel about me, and that's the important thing.'

She slid her arms round her neck and kissed him. 'I love you, Marco, and I'll be proud to be your wife.'

CHAPTER TWELVE

BACK in England, when she was at work Sydney wore her engagement ring on a chain round her neck, tucked underneath her clothes so it was close to her heart. And every time she caught Marco's eye in the department, they shared a private, special smile.

One afternoon in Resus, Sydney had a case where she really needed a more experienced view. She went in search of Marco. 'Can I borrow you for five minutes? I need you to review some X-rays with me, please,' she said.

'Sure.' He came over to the computer with her and she pulled up the files.

'My patient Aiden is a trainee acrobat—he's seventeen years old. He did a handstand yesterday and fell on his left shoulder. It still hurt today, and he said it felt as if everything was pushed forward, so he came in to see us. I put him in a collar to immobilise his neck before sending him to X-ray. It's definitely a broken collarbone, but I'm not happy about treating this one with a sling.' She blew out a breath. 'It's a really bad break.'

He looked at the screen. 'It looks as if the bone's almost through the skin—and if the bone gets exposed to air, he's at risk of getting an infection. You're right.

We can't just strap his arm up, the way we'd normally treat a break there. Call the orthopods and get them to reduce the fracture and pin it.'

'He said his back hurt, so I asked X-ray to do his back as well.' She pulled up the next file. 'Fractured sacral bone, by the look of it.'

'He's not able to train for a couple of months,' Marco said, 'or he's at risk of stopping that fracture healing and making it worse. Have you done a CAT scan to check his neck for injuries?'

'That's happening right now. I wanted to review these X-rays with you while he's in the scanner—the poor kid's had enough waiting about.'

A few minutes later, Aiden was wheeled back in.

'You've definitely broken your collarbone, Aiden, and it's quite a bad break so we're going to need to send you up to the surgeons to have it pinned,' she said. 'The good news is, the scan you just had done shows that there's no injury to your neck, so you're probably feeling the pain from the break rather than anything else.'

'So, once it's pinned, I can go back to training?' he asked.

'Sorry, no,' Marco said. 'You've also fractured your sacral bone, at the base of your spine. So it's not a good idea to train until that's healed, which will be about the same time as the pin's removed from your collarbone—and that will be about nine weeks.'

'Nine weeks?' Aiden looked aghast. 'But the troupe's in a big competition in two weeks' time. I have to be there. It's my big chance. I can't miss it.'

Sydney took his hand and squeezed it. 'If you don't let your bones heal properly, there's a chance you might make things worse—and then it'll take a lot longer to heal. And if the fractures are bad enough, you might never be able to do acrobatics again.'

He went white. 'But—it's all I ever wanted to do. Since I was tiny.'

'I know it's hard,' Marco added, 'but sometimes you have to look at the bigger picture. It's better to miss one opportunity now and then excel at the next one than to try to do things too soon and for it all to go wrong.'

Sydney said quietly, 'I've called the surgeon down, Aiden, so as soon as he's here I'll introduce you to him and he'll talk you through how he's going to pin your collarbone. He won't be long. Is there anything we can get you while you're waiting, and do you want me to call anyone to give you a bit of moral support?'

'I… No. Dad's going to be so mad at me. I've messed up my big chance.'

'You'll get another chance,' she comforted him. 'And your dad's going to be disappointed for you, but I'm sure he's going to be more worried that you're hurt and in pain.'

'You don't know Dad,' Aiden muttered.

Marco frowned. 'Aiden, do you want to talk to us about that fall?'

The boy grimaced. 'What's there to say? I overbalanced and ruined the routine.'

'Did anyone hit you when you made a mistake?' Sydney asked gently, guessing immediately what Marco had been driving at. Was the break from a fall—or from being struck by something?

'No. Dad never uses his fists.' The boy looked shocked enough for her to believe him. 'But words… they stay with you a lot longer. In your head.' Aiden bit his lip. 'He already thinks I'm useless because I'm not as good as he was at my age.'

'Maybe,' Sydney said softly, 'this is a chance to think about what you really want to do. Do you want to be an acrobat for yourself, or just to please your dad? Because you can't live out someone else's dream, love. It won't work, because your heart won't be completely in it, no matter how much you want to please that person.'

'I'm never going to be as good as he was.'

'Then maybe your talents lie in other directions,' Marco said. 'My father was a fashion designer. But I was never interested in clothes, and he was fine about me becoming a doctor.'

'You're lucky,' Aiden said feelingly.

'Can your mum talk to your dad for you?' Sydney asked.

'She went off with someone else. I haven't seen her since I was ten.'

'If you want me to talk to your dad, that's fine,' Marco said. 'And I'll explain to him that if you over-train while you're still healing, you'll never be able to do acrobatics again.'

'And then what will I do?' Aiden asked bleakly. 'I'll have no job, no home—because he's not going to let me stay if I'm not part of the troupe.'

'Maybe we can help with that,' Sydney said. 'I can have a word with social services and see if they can get you somewhere to stay and some careers advice.'

'No. I don't need any of that. I'm going to be an acrobat,' Aiden said, looking panicky.

'OK, love. Try to relax, now. I'll be back to see you in a bit with the surgeon,' Sydney said.

Marco followed her out of Resus. 'Poor kid,' he said. 'That's hard for him, not having anyone he can rely on.'

The same position she'd felt herself to be in, until she'd met Marco.

'Maybe I can have a word with his dad,' he mused.

'This might be one of the things you can't fix,' Sydney warned.

He shrugged. 'Even so, I can try.'

It was one of the things she loved about him: the way he *cared* so much. And if anyone could fix this situation, Marco could.

On the Monday, Max came into work all smiles. 'Carly has a baby brother. Nearly four kilos, mum and baby both doing well—and, no, we still haven't decided on a name.'

'Congratulations,' Marco said, shaking his hand warmly. The more so because he could identify with the relief on Max's face that mother and baby were both fine. It would be the same with him, worrying about Sydney during labour.

'Thanks. If any of you want to go up and visit Marina, I'm sure she'd be delighted to show him off.'

Just as Marco knew that Sydney so desperately wanted to show off their own baby. But she was still keeping things quiet until after the amnio, not wanting to tempt fate. Please, he begged silently. Let this all be OK. For her sake.

'Are you busy at lunchtime?' Sydney asked.

'Not if my favourite doctor wants to have lunch with me.'

'Not *lunch*, exactly,' she said. 'You know I organised the department's collection for the baby?'

'Yes.' He also knew that she was superstitious about things and wouldn't buy a gift until the baby had arrived safely.

'I'm going to buy the baby's present at lunchtime, and I wondered if you wanted to come with me.'

Marco guessed exactly what that was code for. Sydney was itching to look at things for their own baby, but was being equally superstitious and refusing to choose a thing or even decide on a colour for the nursery until they'd had the amnio result. He was in no doubt that she loved their unborn child, but he knew the fear was still holding her back. All he could do was be there, hold her when the doubts got too much for her, and gently remind her that love would get them through anything. 'I'd love to come with you,' he said softly.

He was surprised at how much he enjoyed helping her choose the departmental gifts for Marina and Max's newborn.

'This stuff's so beautiful,' Sydney said wistfully.

'I know, *tesoro*. Not much longer to wait, now. And then you get to do whatever you like with my credit card.'

She laughed. 'But you'll come with me? Help me choose things for our baby?'

He drew her into his arms and kissed her softly. 'I wouldn't miss that for the world.'

At the end of their shift—and when everyone had signed the card and sighed over the gorgeous baby clothes Sydney had chosen—they headed up to the maternity department. Marco held Sydney's hand very tightly as they were let into the ward.

Marina was sitting up in bed, cuddling the baby, when they walked in.

'Hello! Come to see my gorgeous boy and have a cuddle?' she asked.

'You bet.' Sydney handed the parcels to Marco, sat on the bed next to Marina and cradled the baby in her arms.

Marco's heart turned over. He could just see her holding their own baby, her face full of love, and it moved him so much he couldn't speak. He just handed the card and the neatly wrapped gifts to Marina.

'From the department? Oh, thank you!' She opened the parcels, exclaiming in delight over them; but Marco had eyes only for the baby. Ever since the moment he'd seen their baby moving on the screen of the scanner, he melted whenever he was near a baby.

'I always forget how tiny they are when they first arrive,' Marco said, crouching down next to Sydney and touching the baby's hand. How tiny and perfectly formed. The baby yawned, and he couldn't help smiling.

'And how warm they are. That special baby smell,' Sydney said.

He could hear the slight wobble in her voice, and he knew what she was wondering. Was this how it would be for them?

'Do you want to hold him, Marco?' Marina asked.

He couldn't resist. 'Oh, *piccolo*,' he crooned softly, taking the baby from Sydney and cradling him. He knew exactly what Sydney had meant by the warmth, the weight, the special baby smell. And how he wanted to hold his own and Sydney's baby like this. He caught her gaze, and knew she was thinking exactly the same thing. How much she was looking forward to the moment when she first held their baby.

'So how far are you?' Marina asked.

Sydney blinked. 'How far am I what?'

'It's OK. I'm not going to tell anyone. Well, except Max, obviously, but I'll swear him to secrecy,' Marina added. 'Congratulations.'

'How did you know?' Sydney asked.

'The way you held the baby,' Marina said simply. 'The way you looked at each other.'

'It's that obvious?' Marco asked.

'To me, yes, because I've been there myself. I haven't heard any rumours, yet.'

'I'm fourteen weeks,' Sydney said. 'And not really showing that much.' Especially as she was wearing baggy clothes to hide the slight bump.

'The blooming stage.' Marina smiled at her. 'So does that mean we're going to have a departmental wedding?'

'Better come clean,' Marco said ruefully.

Sydney fished out her engagement ring to show Marina. 'Obviously it's against health and safety to wear it at work.'

'And you're keeping it to yourselves for now. Is that why you whisked her off to Italy, Marco?'

'Partly.' Not that he was going to elaborate on the other reason.

'That ring's absolutely gorgeous. Have you set a date?'

'After the baby arrives,' Sydney said. 'We were thinking a spring wedding.'

'It sounds perfect,' Marina said. 'I'm so pleased for you both.'

'Thank you.' Regretfully, Marco handed the baby back to her. 'We'd better let you get some rest.'

'Plus we're being greedy—everyone else in the department is desperate to come up and see you,' Sydney added. She kissed Marina's cheek. 'Well done. He's gorgeous.'

'Irresistible,' Marco agreed, handing the baby back to Marina.

'See you both later,' Marina said with a smile.

Marco took her hand as they left the ward. 'That's going to be us, in a few months. With our own little miracle.' There was a huge lump in his throat. 'I can hardly wait.'

'Me, too,' Sydney said, squeezing his hand. 'Me, too.'

He kissed her. 'We'd better get back to work. I happen to know that Aiden's back in for a check-up this afternoon—and his dad's going to be with him. I think I need to have a word.'

'The man sounds like a complete bully.'

'It's probably insecurity.' Marco shrugged. 'His wife left him, so Aiden's all he has left—and he's probably terrified of losing his son.'

'Which is why he's pushing him away like this, making him feel that he's useless?'

'Some people believe that if you tell someone they're rubbish, they'll fight back to prove you wrong.'

'More like, their self-esteem will drop.'

'But someone who's that scared isn't going to see that. Let's hope he'll listen to me.'

At the end of their shift, Marco and Sydney walked home together, their arms wrapped around each other.

'How did you get on with Aiden's dad?' she asked.

'He just needed someone to point out to him that if he pushed his son any harder right now, Aiden would end up in a wheelchair and resent him for taking away his mobility as well as his career.'

'So he's going to back off?'

Marco nodded. 'I think young Aiden's got the chance now to find out what he really wants to do. If that's acrobatics, fine; if it isn't, he'll still have a home and his dad will support him in whatever he wants to do.'

She stroked his face. 'I'm so glad you're one of life's fixers.'

'Sometimes it works.' He kissed her lightly.

When they made love that night, it was more intense than Sydney had ever felt before. This time, as Marco's body surged into hers, he whispered, 'I love you.'

'I love you too,' she whispered back, adding silently, *for always*.

CHAPTER THIRTEEN

THE day of the amniocentesis, Sydney couldn't concentrate on anything. She put chilli instead of cinnamon on her morning porridge; she stood staring into the fridge, clearly having forgotten what she wanted in the first place; and Marco could barely get a proper sentence out of her.

By the time they got to the waiting room, she was as white as a sheet.

He took her hand. 'Try not to worry, *tesoro*.'

'I can't help it.' She bit her lip. 'And I hope we don't have to wait too much longer. I'm dying to go to the loo, but if I do I'll have to drink more water and we'll have to sit here for another half an hour.'

The receptionist called her name, and she started.

His fingers tightened round hers. 'You're not alone. I'm here,' he said.

'I know.'

But he could feel her shaking.

She lay on the couch, and the ultrasonographer took her hand. 'We're just going to take a tiny bit of amniotic fluid from around the baby so we can grow the cells. You'll just feel a sharp scratch. OK?'

'OK?' she whispered.

'Well done.' The ultrasonographer smeared radio-conductive gel over Sydney's abdomen and then ran the transceiver over it.

Marco glanced at the screen; the baby was moving about a lot, clearly picking up on Sydney's worries.

'Try to relax,' the ultrasonographer said.

But he could see in Sydney's eyes that panic had set in. She was worrying about all the maybes. 'Remember that Sunday morning we walked through Sorrento?' he asked. When she nodded, he began to sing *'Torna a Surriento'*. And eventually the tension in her body seemed to ease and the baby stopped moving about quite so much.

The ultrasonographer inserted the needle and took the fluid. 'All done.' She smiled at Marco. 'You have a lovely voice. Your baby's really going to enjoy bedtime lullabies.'

'So we hear in two weeks?' Sydney asked.

'Two weeks. I'm afraid it does take that long to grow the cells and analyse them.' The ultrasonographer patted her hand. 'I know it's hard, but try not to worry. And try to rest for today and tomorrow, OK?'

Marco took Sydney back to her flat.

'So are you going back to work now?' she asked.

'No. I'm taking the time off with you.'

She frowned. 'Marco, I'm not going to start rushing around doing things.'

'I know, but if you're on your own you'll start brooding. I'm not going to make you have bed rest for the next two days, because I know it'll drive you crazy, but I do want you resting. Put your feet up, *tesoro*. We're going to watch a pile of comedies and play board games and do crosswords together.'

'You're going to keeping me occupied, hmm?'

'As much as I can.' He stroked her face. 'Waiting's the hardest part of anything. But we'll get through this.'

Her face was filled with sadness. 'What if…?'

'We'll deal with it when it comes. Don't build bridges to trouble,' he said softly.

It was easier for both of them to keep their minds occupied at work—until the day when the results were due. They both slept badly the night before, and the atmosphere in the flat was full of tension. Sydney dropped the jar of decaf coffee, which smashed on the kitchen floor; Marco burned the toast; and his jaw ached so much that he was convinced he'd been grinding his teeth in his sleep.

The tension rose with every second that ticked round. When would they get the call?

The phone rang, and she grabbed it. 'Yes. No. Look, I'm sorry, I know you're only doing your job, but I'm perfectly happy with my electricity provider and I'm expecting an important call. Please go away.' She hung up. 'I can't believe I got cold-called today, of all days.'

'They're just doing their job, *tesoro*.'

'If the hospital was trying to ring me when I took that call—'

'Then they'll try your mobile next,' he reminded her.

But her mobile phone didn't ring. And neither did the landline.

Every time they glanced at the clock, thinking that surely a quarter of an hour had passed, they were shocked to discover that it was only a few seconds.

Then the phone rang again. Sydney fumbled as she tried to grab it, dropped the phone and cut off the connection. 'No!' she howled, and checked the display to see who had called.

'Number withheld. It has to be Theo's secretary.'

She rang the number. 'Engaged,' she said, her mouth thinning. She redialled. 'Still engaged.'

'Sydney, if she's talking to someone else, she'll be a couple of minutes. She'll probably try you next,' Marco said gently, trying to calm her down—all this stress wasn't good for her or for the baby.

Sydney redialled again; this time, she got through. 'Hello? It's Sydney Collins. Were you just trying to ring me? Yes.' She paused. 'Yes. I see. Thank you.'

She put the phone down and promptly burst into tears.

'Sydney?' Clearly she'd just heard the news she didn't want to hear. Why else would she be crying her eyes out? Marco wrapped his arms round her. 'Oh, *tesoro*. I know that right now it feels like the end of the world. But we don't have to make any decisions today. We have a little while to work things out.'

'It's OK,' she sobbed. 'It's OK. Chromosome 22. It's *normal*.'

It took a moment for what she's said to sink in.

The baby didn't have NF2.

And then he picked her up, whooped and swung her round in a circle. 'That's fantastic!'

So everything was going to be all right now. Sydney wasn't going to crucify herself any more over whether she'd passed her genetic problem to the baby; now she knew for sure that she hadn't, she could relax into her pregnancy and really enjoy it.

She touched his cheek. 'Marco, you're crying,' she said in wonder.

'Because I'm relieved—not that it would've been a problem for me if the baby had NF2, but because you're not going to blame yourself any more for something that isn't your fault. And I'm happy. And I love you very, very much.'

That weekend, Sydney took Marco to meet her family. And they liked him as much as Marco's family had liked her. Her parents and sisters-in-law were charmed by his good manners, her brothers indulged in good-natured banter about football with him, and her nieces persuaded him to play endless games with them.

'He's lovely,' Sydney's mother said when she managed to get her daughter to herself in the kitchen. 'So much better for you than Craig ever was. Why have you been keeping him a secret all this time?'

'It's complicated,' Sydney hedged. 'And I didn't want to say anything about the baby until I had the amnio results back. Just in case—' her breath caught '—I'd passed on the NF2. I couldn't forgive myself if I had.'

Sydney's mother hugged her. 'Oh, darling. I hate to think that you've been going through all this on your own.'

'I wasn't on my own. Marco supported me.'

'Why didn't you tell me?'

'Because I didn't want to burden you.'

Sydney's mother gave her a rueful smile. 'I'm your mother. You'd never be a burden to me, darling. Though I do understand how you felt—I've been there myself. When you were first diagnosed, your father and I blamed ourselves. I went over and over what had happened when I was pregnant with you, just in case I'd done something that caused it.'

'Mum, it wasn't your fault, or Dad's. It was a genetic mutation. Pure chance.'

'And it wouldn't have been your fault, either, if the baby had it too,' Sydney's mother said softly. 'But I'm glad for your sake that it's all worked out.'

'Me, too,' Sydney said. 'I didn't think it was possible to be this happy.'

Marco's family was equally delighted by the news of the baby and their engagement. When Marco told them, Sydney could hear the shrieks of joy even though he hadn't switched the phone through to speaker mode.

'They want to talk to you,' Marco said with a grin, and handed her the phone.

Ten minutes later, when Sydney hung up, she was slightly dazed.

'What?' Marco asked.

'I think we've just been organised. Your sister's making me a wedding dress and she's flying over next weekend with fabric swatches and designs for me to choose. And, um, your parents and your brother are flying over with her, so they can all meet my family.'

'Ah.' He grimaced. 'Sorry. They're Italian. They like everything big and noisy. I'll tell them to back off.'

She shook her head, smiling. 'No, it's lovely, feeling part of a huge extended family. It was never like that with Craig. It was always made very clear that I was just an in-law.'

'You definitely won't be that with my family. You're one of us,' Marco told her. 'An honorary Italian.'

She smiled back. 'Which is wonderful. Everything's just perfect.'

And it was. Marco's and Sydney's families never

stopped talking the entire weekend, swapping stories and showing each other photographs and laughing. Everyone at work was delighted for them when they announced the news about their engagement and the baby. And when Sydney felt the very first kick inside her, her joy was overwhelming; this was everything she wanted. Just perfect.

Until she became aware that her hearing had dulled rapidly on her left side. She could only work out what patients were saying if they were close to her—and noisy social situations were next to impossible.

She tried telling herself that it was winter, she had a bit of a cold and it was just slightly inflamed Eustachian tubes affecting her hearing; but when she heard the soft, high-pitching ringing in her ears, she knew.

Tinnitus.

So the schwannomas on her vestibular nerves were growing and starting to cause problems.

That evening, after work, she sat on the sofa next to Marco and took his hand. 'We need to talk.'

He frowned. 'What's up?'

'I have a problem.'

He scooped her onto his lap and rested his hand on her bump. 'What kind of problem, *tesoro*?'

'I'm getting tinnitus. I think… I think it's the vestibular schwannomas. They must've grown and started pressing on the nerves.'

He stroked her face. 'So would that be part of the reason why you slept through the alarm this morning?'

'I *was* tired and I slept like a log last night. But…' She sighed. She had to be honest with him. 'I probably didn't hear the alarm. I had a patient today—I couldn't hear half of what he was saying. It didn't help that Cubicles were particularly noisy and his voice was soft. And I do have a bit of a cold. It might be just that.'

'But you're worried, and that's enough for me. We'll see Michael and find out what's going on and what the options are.'

She bit her lip. 'I can't help remembering what Craig said—that I'm selfish for wanting this baby, knowing that the pregnancy hormones can make my condition worse.'

Marco said something very pithy about Craig. 'You're not selfish at all. Look, your NF2 is part of you, and we're in this together. It doesn't change the way I feel about you or about our baby. He wasn't planned, but he's very much wanted.'

'I know.'

'But sometimes it's hard to forget the most hurtful words,' he said. He kissed her swiftly. 'Thank you for trusting me. For not shutting me out.'

'I might have to rely on you quite a lot,' she warned.

'I'll be here.' He kissed her again. 'Always.'

To her relief, Michael fitted them in the next day. 'We can do an MRI of your head and it won't affect the baby,' he reassured her. 'And we need to do some acoustic tests to see how badly your hearing's been affected.'

But his face was grim as he showed them the results on his computer screen after the scan. 'Bad news, I'm afraid, Sydney. The left schwannoma is growing faster than the right. You're going to need surgery—either through microsurgery or gamma knife—or you risk losing your hearing in that ear completely if the tumour puts too much pressure on the acoustic nerve and damages it.'

'I'm not having surgery while I'm pregnant—and absolutely no to the gamma knife.' She blew out a breath. 'I won't expose the baby to radiation.' She lifted her chin. 'I had months of worrying myself sick over whether the baby's inherited my NF2. I'm not going to spend the rest of my pregnancy worrying over whether the baby's been affected by anaesthetic or radiation or anything else.'

'It's Sydney's call,' Marco said. 'I'm backing whatever decision she makes.'

'I'll be fine. If the worst comes to the worst, I still have hearing in my right ear. And maybe we can use the gamma knife to shrink the tumour after the baby's born,' Sydney said.

Michael nodded. 'OK. We'll keep monitoring you. In the meantime, try not to worry.'

Afterwards, Sydney bit her lip. 'Did I do the right thing, Marco? Should I have opted for surgery?'

'*Tesoro*, it's your call,' he said gently. 'You know the risks and you know the options. I meant what I said. Whatever you want to do, I'll back you all the way.'

'If I lose my hearing…' She dragged in a breath. 'I think we should get a baby listener with flashing lights, so I can see when the baby's crying if I can't hear.'

'For during the day, that's a good idea. At night. I'll wake, so you don't need to worry,' Marco said. He stroked her hair. 'What about your back? I've noticed you standing with your hands pressed into the small of your back.'

She smiled. 'That's something that just about every pregnant woman does. It's completely normal pregnancy backache. And, believe me, I remember what the other sort of back pain felt like,' she said feelingly, 'so I know the difference. I'm fine. It's just my hearing.'

Just. She was so brave, Marco thought. And he was incredibly proud of her.

To both Marco and Sydney's relief, the rest of her pregnancy passed without any more complications. Sydney's hearing worsened a fair bit more, but she had no other worrying symptoms.

Two days before the baby was due, she woke in the night, feeling slightly uncomfortable. She managed to turn over and go back to sleep, but by breakfast-time she realised what was happening. 'Marco, the baby's coming.'

'Contractions?' He went white. 'How often?'

'Twenty minutes apart. I think.'

'I'll ring the hospital.' He punched in Theo's number; the conversation was brief, and then he rang Ellen to say he needed cover for the day because he was going to be at Sydney's side for every second of labour. 'Theo says come in when your contractions are every ten minutes, and Ellen sends her love,' he reported.

Gradually over the morning, the contractions drew closer together. The second they were ten minutes apart, Marco drove Sydney in to the hospital.

'OK?' he asked as they headed into the maternity unit.

She nodded.

He could tell by her expression that she was being brave. 'You're nervous, *tesoro.*'

'I know we did all the classes and we know all the breathing, but...'

'It will be fine,' he reassured her. 'And I'm not leaving your side.'

'I'm excited as well as nervous. I can't *wait* to meet our baby,' Sydney said.

He smiled. 'Me, too.'

Theo examined her, did a quick check of the baby's heartbeat, then smiled in satisfaction. 'Everything's fine. I'll leave you in the capable hands of Iris, our senior midwife. Any worries, call me.'

Marco rubbed her back with every contraction and got her walking around the ward. And then finally Sydney was ready to go into the delivery suite. Marco coached her through the breathing and made no protest when she gripped his hands and dug her nails in.

'One last push,' Iris encouraged. And then they heard a cry and she smiled. 'You have a beautiful baby boy.'

'Niccolo,' Sydney said. 'His name's Niccolo.'

Iris weighed him and checked him over. 'Perfect Apgar score,' she said as she handed the baby back to Sydney.

Sydney was so tired—and yet so happy at the same time. She wanted to yell from the rooftops how happy she was, even abseil down the tower of the London Victoria. And the sudden rush of love she felt for their baby was stronger than she would ever have believed.

Marco's eyes were glittering with unshed tears; she knew that, like hers, they were happy tears.

'He's so beautiful. He looks like you,' she said softly.

'Our little miracle. I'm so proud of you both.' His voice was thick with emotion. 'I love you, Sydney.'

Once they were back on the ward, there seemed to be a constant stream of visitors wanting to congratulate them and see their beautiful baby. Sydney's entire family; Max and Marina; Theo and his wife, Maddie; Michael; and every doctor and nurse from the emergency department. So much love and so many good wishes for them, Sydney thought happily. It just didn't get any better than this.

CHAPTER FOURTEEN

SYDNEY had agreed with Michael that a month after her son was born she'd have the gamma knife operation on the tumour. Fergus Keating had asked one of his former colleagues, Amy Ashby, to come to London and help with the operation; Amy was an expert in gamma knife surgery and had set up a specialist neurology treatment centre in Norfolk. Sydney liked her immediately. 'I feel safe in your hands,' she said.

'Good. That's how it should be.' Amy looked thoughtful. 'Sydney, I have to be honest with you—I can't promise it's going to do the trick and get your hearing back completely. If there's too much damage to the nerve, you might need an auditory brainstem implant before you can hear properly again on that side. But I'm hoping that in a couple of weeks' time you'll have healed enough for it to make a difference.'

'That's good enough for me,' Sydney said.

The day after the operation, Marco strolled into his wife's hospital room, carrying the baby in his arms. 'I think Mamma might just be ready to come home, Nico,' he told the baby.

Sydney was sitting on the bed, case packed, tapping her fingers impatiently. 'I've been ready for *hours*.'

'Sorry. Somebody wanted his breakfast. He yelled the place down because I wasn't heating the milk fast enough for him. And *then* he decided to be contrary and take his time about drinking it. Apparently I'm not as good as you, when it comes to breakfast.'

He handed the baby over to Sydney, and she held him close, breathing in his scent. 'Oh, I missed you, *bambino*,' she said softly. 'And I missed your daddy. I could've come home last night, but, oh, no. Daddy said I had to stay in, just in case.'

'Easier than having to rush you here in an ambulance,' Marco said dryly.

'There was no need to be so cautious. I was fine. Amy and Fergus are brilliant surgeons. I can go back to completely normal activities today.' She gave him a rueful smile. 'Though I will admit to having a bit of a headache.'

'You had a cage screwed to your head and then radiation beams zapping you. Of course you have a headache.'

'The cage bit was done under an LA, so it didn't hurt, and I didn't feel a thing during the gamma knife stuff.' She rolled her eyes. 'You know that. You were there with me.' She kissed the baby. 'Nico, Daddy's such a fusspot.'

'Of course Daddy fusses. You're both important,' Marco informed the baby. He sat down next to Sydney and kissed her. 'Have they given you anything for that headache, *tesoro*?'

'Yes. I'm just waiting for Fergus to sign the discharge form.' She bit her lip. 'When he and Amy called in to check up on me last night, after you left, they had a chat with me about the scan. They say my left vestibular nerve is too damaged for me to get much of my hearing back in that ear, but they're confident the right-hand schwannoma's going to shrink over the next couple of months—enough for me to hear really well again in my right ear.'

'That's a bonus.' He stroked her cheek. 'We'll manage just fine with Nico. And there's always the possibility of an ABI later for your left ear.'

She nodded. 'I'd hate not to be able to hear Nico's first words properly.'

'You will,' he promised. 'And think of all the other firsts we have to look forward to. The first tooth, the first steps, the first day at school, the first driving lesson...'

She laughed, just as Marco had intended her to. 'I'm surprised you didn't go up to the first grandchild!'

'That, too. We have *plans*. A whole lovely life ahead of us.' Marco stole a kiss. 'I'm going to see where Fergus has got to. And then we're going home. The three of us.'

Their wedding day was the brightest day in May that Sydney could ever remember. She was full of smiles as she arrived at the register office in the car with her father. She and Marco had arranged with the registrar to be interviewed separately before the ceremony, because both of them wanted to stick to the tradition of not seeing each other on their wedding day until the wedding itself.

'OK, love?' her father asked.

She smiled. 'More than OK. I don't think I've ever been this happy.'

The beautiful white stone building with its imposing steps, moulded doorway and filigree work in the arch above the double doors was familiar to her from newspaper photographs of the rich and famous. As she drew nearer she could see that there were rose petals scattered on the steps; clearly someone had already been married here today, starting a new life together full of hope. Just as she and Marco were facing a new life together full of hope.

She sorted out all her side of the paperwork with the registrar while the guests were being seated, and then it was time for her to enter the room. Both their families were there waiting for them, along with their closest friends—including Marco's, who'd flown over from Italy with his family.

She'd forgotten that Marco's friends had been in a band with him in their student days—but they'd brought guitars with them, and performed a quiet, acoustic version of 'Walking on Sunshine' as she entered the room. The song he'd used to sing her down from the abseil, the very first time they'd met—and so appropriate, because that was exactly what it felt like as she walked towards him. When he turned round to watch her walk towards him, the sheer love on his face made her heart skip a beat.

Both of them meant every word when they made their vows.

When the registrar gave him permission to kiss his bride, he kissed her lingeringly. 'I love you. And you've just made me the happiest man in the world.'

There was a huge lump in her throat, but she managed to say, 'And I love you, too, Marco. So much.'

The wedding meal at the hotel they'd booked was

wonderful—the room was full of laughter and smiles, and there was none of the awkwardness between the different sides of the family that she'd noticed at weddings she'd been to in the past. The evening reception was a lot bigger; in the emergency department, you got to know so many people from other departments, and it seemed that half the hospital wanted to share their day.

'Time to hit the dance floor,' Marco said.

The song they'd chosen was the one Marco had played to her about how amazing he thought she was. And it was even better because she could hear him clearly, thanks to the gamma knife surgery. She wasn't going to miss a single tiny bit of her wedding day.

'You're amazing, too,' she whispered at the end, and kissed him.

She paced herself with the dancing during the evening, but towards the end she was starting to feel tired. She didn't admit it, but Marco clearly noticed.

'Time to sneak off, *tesoro*,' he said.

'Don't we have to say goodbye to everyone first?'

'It'll take the rest of the night to do that. Everyone will understand.' He smiled at her. 'And I kind of want you to myself. Especially as Nico has two sets of grandparents on hand to spoil him—and we have the honeymoon suite.'

A ripple of desire slid down her spine at the expression in his eyes. 'Now, that sounds tempting…'

When they reached their room, he opened the door, then picked her up to carry her over the threshold, letting the door click closed behind them. He set her back on her feet in front of the four-poster bed and turned the lights to low.

'You look lovely, *tesoro*.'

'Thanks to your talented sister.'

'Not just the dress. You look lovely anyway. And now you're all mine.' He took off her bolero jacket and hung it up, then slowly unzipped her dress, kissing every inch of skin he uncovered. And Sydney didn't flinch when he finally removed her dress, baring her arm, because she knew that he loved her exactly as she was. The lumpy skin was no longer a badge to remind her not to trust. It was just a part of her—and Marco's love had taught her to accept that.

She thoroughly enjoyed undressing him, too. 'I see what you mean. You looked stunning in that suit—but it's just window-dressing. Because you're gorgeous anyway.'

'You've made me so happy,' he said, holding her close. 'I love you, Dr Ranieri.'

She loved the sound of her new name on his lips. 'I love you, too, Dr Ranieri. For the rest of our days.'

* * * * *

A sneaky peek at next month...

MODERN™

INTERNATIONAL AFFAIRS, SEDUCTION & PASSION GUARANTEED

My wish list for next month's titles...

In stores from 16th September 2011:

☐ The Most Coveted Prize – Penny Jordan

☐ The Night that Changed Everything – Anne McAllister

☐ The Lost Wife – Maggie Cox

☐ Weight of the Crown – Christina Hollis

☐ Bought: His Temporary Fiancée – Yvonne Lindsay

In stores from 7th October 2011:

☐ The Costarella Conquest – Emma Darcy

☐ Craving the Forbidden – India Grey

☐ Heiress Behind the Headlines – Caitlin Crews

☐ Innocent in the Ivory Tower – Lucy Ellis

Available at WHSmith, Tesco, Asda, Eason, Amazon and Apple

Just can't wait?

  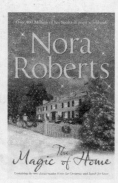

New Voices is back!

New Voices
returns on
13th September 2011!

For sneak previews and exclusives:

 Like us on facebook.com/romancehq

 Follow us on twitter.com/MillsandBoonUK

Last year your votes helped Leah Ashton win
New Voices 2010 with her fabulous story
Secrets & Speed Dating!

Who will you be voting for this year?

Visit us Online

Find out more at
www.romanceisnotdead.com

NEW_VOICES

New Voices
MILLS & BOON
Starts 13th September!

Top Writing Tips from Mills & Boon Editors

We're looking for talented new authors and if you've got a romance bubbling away in your head we want to hear from you! But before you put pen to paper, here are some top tips…

Understand what our readers want: Do your research! Read as many of the current titles as you can and get to know the different series with our guidelines on www.millsandboon.co.uk.

Love your characters: Readers follow their emotional journey to falling in love. Focus on this, not elaborate, weird and wonderful plots.

Make the reader want to walk in your heroine's shoes: She should be believable, someone your reader can identify with. Explore her life, her triumphs, hopes, dreams. She doesn't need to be perfect—just perfect for your hero…she can have flaws just like the rest of us!

The reader should fall in love with your hero! Mr Darcy from *Pride and Prejudice*, Russell Crowe in *Gladiator* or Daniel Craig as James Bond are all gorgeous in different ways. Have your favourite hero in mind when you're writing and get inspired!

Emotional conflict: Just as real-life relationships have ups and downs, so do the heroes and heroines in novels. Conflict between the two main characters generates emotional and sensual tension.

Have your say or enter New Voices at:
www.romanceisnotdead.com

Visit us Online

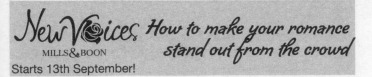

Avoiding the dreaded cliché

Open your story book with a bang—hook your reader in on the first page and show them instantly that this story is unique.

A successful writer can use a conventional theme and twist it to deliver something with real wow factor!

Once you've established the direction of your story, bring in fresh takes and new twists to these traditional storylines.

Here are four things to remember:

- Stretch your imagination
- Stay true to the genre
- It's all about the characters—start with them, not the plot!
- M&B is about creating fantasy out of reality. Surprise us with your characters, stories and ideas!

So whether it's a marriage of convenience story, a secret baby theme, a traumatic past or a blackmail story, make sure you add your own unique sparkle which will make your readers come back for more!

Good luck with your writing!

We look forward to meeting your fabulous heroines and drop-dead gorgeous heroes!

# *Have Your Say*

You've just finished your book.
So what did you think?

We'd love to hear your thoughts on our
'Have your say' online panel
www.millsandboon.co.uk/haveyoursay

- 🌹 Easy to use
- 🌹 Short questionnaire
- 🌹 Chance to win Mills & Boon® goodies

 Visit us Online Tell us what you thought of this book now at
www.millsandboon.co.uk/haveyoursay

YOUR_SAY